# PRAISE

Brock Adams' first collection of fiction is fresh, witty, and perceptive. These seventeen stories, set mostly in the American South, explore relationships in which trust and identity are called into question. The characters are plausible and engaging, the plots are full of surprises, and the details are beautifully drawn.

*Gulf* explores a range of relationships: between men and women; grandparents, fathers, brothers, and sons; tourists and natives, and between the old and the young. It isn't afraid to depart from realism from time to time to explore abstractions, but it does so vividly and convincingly. Sparkling dialogue and a touch of the absurd enliven mundane situations and make fantastic ones entirely believable.

A real pleasure to read, Adams' stories will linger with readers long after they've finished this book.

-Susan Hubbard, author of *Blue Money*


Brock Adams as a young man seemed conservative, almost square. There is nothing about him square now. In this work there is plenty of the new weird, but it strangely rests on an old-feeling heroic moral ethos that is damned nigh Hemingwayey. Mr. Adams's career as a writer promises us something interesting to watch.

-Padgett Powell, author of *Edisto*

# GULF

A Collection of Short Stories by

BROCK ADAMS

Pocol Press
Clifton, VA

POCOL PRESS

Published in the United States of America
by Pocol Press
6023 Pocol Drive
Clifton VA 20124
www.pocolpress.com

Publisher's Cataloguing-in-Publication

Adams, Brock, 1982-

  Gulf : a collection of short stories / Brock Adams. – 1st ed. –
  Clifton, VA : Pocol Press, c2010.

  p. ; cm.

  ISBN: 978-1-929763-44-3

  1. Interpersonal relations—Fiction. 2. Identity (Psychology)—
Fiction. 3. Mexico, Gulf of—Fiction. 4. Short stories, American. I. Title

PS3601.D368 G85 2010
813.6--dc22                                    1004

Cover painting is the Gulf of Mexico from Shell Island, near Panama
City, Florida. Painted by author's grandmother, Martha Brock, in 1995.

# PUBLISHING HISTORY

"Burn." *Acapella Zoo*. 2009.
"Holiday." *Muscadine Line: A Southern Journal*. 25
      (January-March 2009).
"Google Earth." *Root*. Winter 2008.
"Things You Can Do With a Can of Campbell's Soup."
      *Barrelhouse*. Fall 2008 Online Issue.
"Blue Morning Dark." *Café Irreal* 27. (Summer 2008).
"People I'll Never See Again." *The Scruffy Dog Review*.
      Summer 2008.
"Audacious." *The Cypress Dome* 19. (Spring 2008).
"Fragile." *The Cypress Dome* 19. (Spring 2008).
"Gulf." *Eureka Literary Magazine* 15.2. (Spring, 2007): 44-46.

# AWARDS

"Audacious"; second prize; *Playboy*'s College Fiction
      Contest 2008.
"Bloodhound"; third prize; Hub City Creative Writing
      Contest for Fiction.

Dedicated to my Grandfather, Lester C. Brock

## ACKNOWLEDGMENTS

I would like to thank my thesis advisor, Susan Hubbard, for her tireless and spirited guidance during the creation of this collection. She has been a mentor and a friend.

Thanks to Don Stap and Pat Rushin, the other two members of my thesis committee, and all the other faculty and staff at UCF who have made my graduate experience memorable.

A special thanks to two of my best readers: my wife Jill, and my mother Angie Adams. Additional thanks to my Dad and my brother John, my grandparents, and all the other relatives and friends who have been there for me over the past twenty-seven years. I wouldn't be the person that I am without you.

# TABLE OF CONTENTS

*The dark water of the true gulf is the greatest healer that there is.*

-Ernest Hemingway
*The Old Man and the Sea*

# BURN

She's left her hair curler burning on the bathroom counter again, and this time, when I stumble in the dark and rest my hand on the counter while I'm peeing, I wrap my palm around the searing metal. I'm holding it there for a second before I realize what's happening; it's long enough for the skin to singe and the pain to travel up the long nerves and into my brain, enough time for me to say something like *Yeeeeeeoooooooooooow* before I yank my arm back and the curler clatters on the tile.

*Why was she curling her hair, anyway?*

It's immediately obvious that I'm going to lose that skin. It's pale and papery where I grabbed the iron, an inch and a half of cooked epidermis in the center of my palm. I pick at it with my fingernail; the skin peels away like cellophane off a piece of meat. Underneath, the new skin is white and slick. Not ready for the sun.

*She curls her hair when she wants to look pretty. Curls the ends, inward, a wave in toward her neck.*

In the shower the rest of the skin comes off under the washcloth. It splats lightly on the tile and crinkles and drifts in the water, disappears down the drain. The bare skin on my hand stings under the water, ten thousand sunburns compressed into something the size of the cap of a pen. The new skin is pure, glowing and moon-colored, surrounded by tan and roughness. It's a part of my body I'm not supposed to see. I force myself to stop staring.

Dried off and back in the medicine cabinet, searching for Band-aids. There's some on the top shelf, behind the sunscreen. They're Scooby Doo brand. I cover the burn up with a blue bandage with Velma on it.

I read in bed until Kitty comes home. It's 3:15 in the morning when I hear the door open and close. She clomps across the floor in the other room. She's trying to be quiet but she's still loud; she's wearing her high heels. She pokes her head in the door.

"I didn't know you were still awake," she says.

She's wearing deep red lipstick. It's too dark for her fair skin. It's almost as red as her hair. Her hair is curled in toward her neck.

"Was just waiting up on you," I say.

1

"You shouldn't have." She disappears, more clomping.

I put my book in the drawer beside the bed. "I was starting to get worried."

"I was just at the library," she calls from the kitchen. The refrigerator opens and its cold electrical sound fills the room. "I told you that. I was studying." She comes back into the bedroom and kicks her shoes off in the corner. She's quiet now that she's barefoot. She pads into the bathroom.

*The library's not open this late.*

"Library closes at one," I say. "I was getting worried."

"They were open late for exams."

"Really?"

"Did you cut yourself?" she says. She stands in the doorway of the bathroom with the Scooby Doo box in her hand.

"Burn," I say. I turn the light off and roll up in the covers. "From your curler."

"Oh, baby," she says. She climbs onto the bed. "I left it on again?"

I nod.

"I'm so sorry. Let me see."

I pull my hand out from under the covers and hold it out at her. She pulls the fingers open like the tendrils of an anemone; she kisses the Band-aid. Her lips feel like wet marshmallows. "Better?" she says.

"A little."

She goes back into the bathroom and runs the water for a bit. She brushes her teeth. Washes off her makeup. She puts on one of my t-shirts and climbs into bed with me. We say goodnight. We're silent for ten minutes. Then she gets up.

"Where are you going?"

"I have to call my sister," she says. She's pulling on a pair of shorts. "I forgot I told her I'd call her."

*Her sister works early. She won't be up this late.*

She pulls her cell phone from her purse and slips on her sandals and goes outside. She doesn't come back for an hour and a half.

In the morning I tear the Band-aid off slowly. It takes a bunch of dead skin with it. The burn looks worse than the night before. It's turned scabby, but not a hard, healing scab–everything is still wet and gross. The bright white is covered in crusty browns and squishy reds. It looks like chopped-up bacon. It looks bigger than it did last night.

*It just looks bigger because of the scabbing.*

I put a new Band-aid on it. In this one, Shaggy and Scooby are running from a bedsheet ghost. I wrap my hand in a strip of white medical tape to keep the Band-aid in place.

Kitty is still in bed while I get dressed. She's breathing loud and raspy, something just below a snore. Her mouth is slightly open, slightly smiling.

At work, the boss wanders by my desk around the same time every morning. "Cute Band-aid," he says today. "Are you ten years old?"

"It's all we had," I say.

"What did you do?"

"Burned myself. Kitty left the curling iron on."

"What a bitch."

There's brown around the edges of the Band-aid by the end of the day. When I pull it off, the burn is wider, longer, deeper. It takes two Band-aids to cover it.

*It just looks bigger because it's healing.*

Kitty comes home after three again. I'm on the couch when she opens the door. She doesn't have her books with her.

"I was studying online," she says.


In the morning the Band-aids have fallen off because the skin they were stuck to is gone. I close the door to the bathroom and turn on the lights. The fluorescents hum. The incandescents burn yellow. The wound takes up most of the inside of my hand, stretching out over and around the fingertips, up in a shock of red on my wrist and forearm.

The edges are red and raw. The skin is grainy and a million shades of rust.

The burn is long and deep now, a hole in my arm. It's like someone scooped me out with a melon baller. At the center of the burn, at the deepest point in the middle of my palm, there's something smooth and hard and red. I wipe the red away; it's shiny white underneath. Polished bone.

3

I've lost a couple of fingernails. My feet are itchy.

I wrap everything up in gauze and get into the shower. I try to keep my arm dry. Wash with one hand.

There's a trickle of blood running to the drain.

*It's bleeding now. Shit.*

The gauze is still pure white. No blood. The blood on the tile is a burning red streamer from the drain to my foot. There's something in the drain, some flesh-colored nub.

*That's not my toe. That's not my fucking toe.*

I get down on one knee and pull it out of the drain. It's my little toe.

In the next room, Kitty is talking in her sleep.

The boss stares at me. He wrings his hands.

*Just let me do my job.*

"You okay?" he says.

"Yeah," I say. "Why?"

"You just look kind of, you know, sickly." He looks around the office. "You don't have anything contagious, do you?"

"I just burned myself."

"But your other arm."

I look at my left arm. There are two new burns, one near my wrist, the size of a quarter, and another one wrapping its way around my biceps. They start to hurt as soon as I look at them.

"Damn curling irons," I say.

"Your nose."

"What?"

*I smell copper.*

He pulls a handkerchief from his pocket and hands it to me. I put it to my nose and it comes away red. Blood flows freely, over my lips, onto my shirt.

"I think you should take the rest of the day off," the boss says.

Kitty is going to be waiting for me at the restaurant. It's date night.

It takes the better part of the afternoon to wrap the burns. The grandaddy burn, the first one, runs from the middle of my palm all the way up and over my shoulder. It's ragged at the

4

edges. I pick at a piece of skin near my collarbone and give it a tug; it peels off in a long smooth sheet from my right shoulder to my left hip. That wet, bare white skin is under it, a stripe like a sash across my chest. There's more new burns–one under my left nipple, a crescent shaped one on my stomach, several little ones dotted on the tops of my legs.

*And the other toes. The other two that came off in my shoes, at some point.*

It takes four rolls of gauze to cover everything up. I'm wrapped head to toe. Good God, like a burn victim.

I wear my winter clothes out to dinner, even though it's summer. Everything is covered, except for the part on my palm and a stab of red on my neck, a feeler creeping up from the wound across my chest. I keep my fist clenched. Outside, the evening's covered in that midsummer, late-day sunlight that turns everything gold. I walk to the restaurant. It hurts to walk. My legs don't fit right in my hips.

She's at the table, on the phone, laughing into the phone. Her hair isn't curled. She hangs up when she sees me.

"Why are you wearing that?" she says.

"I didn't want to sport the Scooby Doo Band-aid at dinner," I say. "And I like this shirt. You don't like this shirt?"

"It looks ridiculous." She looks at her menu. We don't talk. The waiter takes our orders and leaves.

"How's the studying going?" I say.

"Okay."

"When are your exams?"

"I have one on Thursday and one on Friday." She taps her finger on her glass and swirls the water with her straw. She looks around the restaurant, out the window.

"You think you'll do well?" I say. My back is itching, stinging.

*New burns are opening up.*

"Where are our salads?" she says.

*I'm going to be more scab than skin.*

She keeps looking out the window. She takes her phone from her purse and looks at it. She drinks all the water in the glass.

The waiter brings the salads. I pick up my fork and stab a piece of lettuce and my ring finger comes off and lands next to a cherry tomato. Kitty is looking at her plate, mixing the dressing with the vegetables.

*Tell her it's an anchovy. Tell her it's a big crouton.*

She doesn't see. I put the finger in my pocket. She looks up and I smile at her. She goes back to eating.

Her phone rings. "Be right back," she says. She goes outside with the phone.

My teeth feel loose. I can wiggle each one of them with my tongue.

My tongue is loose, too.

She comes back in and stands by the table. "I have to go," she says. I nod. "Just stay up tonight. I won't be home too late." She looks around the room. Bites her lip. "We need to have a talk."

I give her a four-fingered wave, but she's already gone.

The sun is going down when I get home. I sit on the couch and watch the square of liquid-orange sunlight slide across the floor and up the wall. It's getting dark, so I get up to flip the switch by the door and turn on the light. I take a step and my right foot stays behind, sitting all alone where I left it. So I hop to the light switch and back on my left foot and collapse back into the couch. I turn on the TV.

*I'm coming apart.*

My lost foot is collapsing in on itself. It's falling into the shoe. Like a sandcastle in the rising tide. It's a lump, now it's just brownish grainy stuff on the inside of the shoe. I pick up the shoe. It's empty.

*Disappearing.*

I try to pick up the remote, but my hand breaks off at the wrist. There's no pain, just a short cracking sound, and some dust that rises and drifts through the waning sunlight and vanishes. The gauze slowly unravels, falls like ticker-tape to the floor. I can't even turn my head to look at what's underneath. I swallow my teeth, one at a time.

Then the room jolts, jars, tilts forward, bounces and spins. I see the couch and my shoes and the bottom of the coffee table, then the floor, then the couch again, and the room rolls by, then slows, rocks, and is still. I'm under the TV stand. It doesn't make sense. I can't fit under the TV stand.

*My eyes can fit under the TV stand.*

From where my eyes end up I can see my body on the couch. My legs are unmaking themselves from the ankles up, the skin and sinew and bone trickling like sand through the cracks in the floor. My body is still and hollow. My mouth and my eye sockets are dark holes in my head.

*And Kitty was right. That shirt looks ridiculous.*

The floor is dirty, dusty. It's easy to see that from here. I watch as my pants flatten and collapse while the legs drift away; my watch tinks on the floor when the wrist goes. My head tilts further and further forward until it comes loose and lands in my lap, then melts into the folds of the couch cushions.

After a while there's nothing on the couch but clothes.

Nothing happens for a long time.

Then Kitty comes home. She's on the phone. "Yeah, I'm here now. I'm going to tell him," she says. She hangs up. She calls my name. Walks from room to room.

I try to get her attention.

She pauses in the bedroom. She dials her phone, puts it to her ear, taps her foot. "He's not here," she says. She comes into the living room and stands right in front of the TV stand. Her feet are too big for her high heels. "No, no. I'm not waiting on him. I don't know where he is. He left his shit all over the couch."

She walks back to the door. I try to wink, blink, or bat my eyelashes, squint or roll or cross my eyes or anything to get her attention, but eyes don't do much when they're not in your head. So I stare daggers, I burn cold holes into the side of her head.

*She always loved my eyes.*

"Fuck it," she says into the phone. "No. You don't need to come over here. I'm taking my stuff. He'll figure it out." She hangs up the phone and puts it in her purse. She clomps around the house, taking pictures off the shelves, CDs off the rack, putting them all in her purse. It's a big purse. She goes into the other room and shuffles through the drawers. Then she's back in the living room. I want her to see me so bad.

*She loved my eyes. Said they looked like the big sky in Colorado. Like clean swimming pools.*

7

Kitty looks around the room; her eyes fall on the shirt on the couch. It's moving, twitching. She picks it up and reaches her hand inside. I can feel her on me, electric and cold and firm. She throws the shirt away and holds my heart in her hand. From under the TV stand, the heart looks small and sad, like something you pull out of a turkey before you cook it. She holds it to the light and looks at it, hefts it like she's checking out tomatoes at the supermarket. It beats its weak beat in her grip. She opens her purse and puts it inside. Then she walks out the door and flips off the light.

The room is dark. I feel my pupils dilating. They get wider, the blackness spreading like an inkspill across the blue of the iris. The black crosses the borders of the cornea and spreads over the white; my eyes darken until there's nothing left but black, black like nighttime on the bottom of the ocean, like a hole cut in the far side of outer space.

# GULF

He's getting too red. Maybe not. He's flecked with sand, silhouetted against the sun and the green of the Gulf. He can wait a little longer. Next time he comes up, dry him off and put another coat of sun screen on him.

He's looking at the yellow plastic cup in my hand. The ice is melting in the cup. My sweet tea tastes dirty and old.

"Mommy? Mommy, can I have that cup?" he asks.

"What for?"

"I want to make towers." He points at his sand castle, squat and brown near the water.

Jake leans toward me and opens the ice chest that separates our folding chairs. He takes the lid off and pulls another cup, a blue one, from the plastic sleeve and hands it to our son, who sprints back to the water's edge. Jake fishes another Corona out of the ice. He braces the edge of the bottlecap on the side of his folding chair and pops his palm against the top; the cap flies off and he holds the bottle wet and lidless in his hand.

"Hand me a lime?" Jake says.

I'm watching our son. He's packing wet sand into the cup and upending it on the corners of his castle. Some of the towers stand firm. Some crumble. Jake sighs and pulls a lime wedge out of the ice chest, smushes it into the bottle's neck. He puts the lid on the chest and leans back. His eyes are closed and he dangles the beer from two fingers.

"When do you want to tell him?" he says.

A drip sweats from my cup and splats on my leg. The tea is warm. Leafy junk drifts at the bottom. "Next week," I say. "Let him enjoy this."

Jake is scratching his leg. He's getting sunburned. His body isn't used to the sun anymore.

His skin used to turn brown instead of red, back when we first got married and he came home tan and smelling of shrimp and salt from his day on the boat. When his body was hard and lean and muscles snaked all the way up his arms when he brushed his fingers over my legs. When he climbed on top of me covered in grime and I breathed in the seaweed smell because neither of us could stand to wait for him to take a shower. In the tiny warm

9

apartment, we fell asleep just as the stars came out. He'd be back on the boat before the birds woke up.

Jake sips his beer. "I'm going to have to come visit him," he says. "I don't think it's right for him to stay with me and Alice. At least not at first."

"Probably not." There's a band with steel drums playing at the restaurant on the pier. Jimmy Buffet songs float in the wind. Someone is frying catfish. The Gulf is flat, like a brimfull bowl of green Jell-o. A shirtless man in cutoff blue jeans kneels in the sand beside my son, talks to him. The man is old. His skin is so tan and leathery that it looks bruised, almost blue. He is smiling and my son is smiling.

"Do you think you can stand that?" Jake says.

"What?"

"Me staying with you. To visit him. I could sleep on the pullout."

"It will be fine."

Jake tilts the bottle back and spills the beer. It pools at the top of his gut. His breasts are nearly as big as mine.

College had softened him. Work turned him to mush. The callouses that scratched my skin disappeared when he switched from nets to a keyboard. He started going to bed late. He was a different man when the stars were out. He needed a different woman.

"You're being very civil about this," Jake says. "I really appreciate it. You could have handled it differently. This could be much harder on him."

The old man pulls a Swiss Army knife from his pocket. My son looks at it, wide-eyed. The man opens one blade at a time. He uses a large one to cut windows into the towers, then he folds it shut. He takes the paring blade and carves spiked barricades along the castle walls.

"How do you think he'll handle it?" Jake says.

The old man opens the knife's bottle opener and lets my son press the hook-shaped pattern into the doors and the windows. The man sees me watching him and smiles. I wave a finger at him.

"Do you think he'll be okay?" Jake goes on, "I mean, some kids get royally screwed up. My friend Chris–remember Chris?– he was never the same." He finishes his beer and drops the bottle in the sand beside the other three. I can feel him looking at me. "I think he'll be okay," he says. "He's a tough kid."

Waves are building along the shore and for some reason I think of a story my grandmother told me. She said that her grandmother told the story to her. When she was a child and they lived in Pass Christian, right on the Gulf in Mississippi long before there were any condos or highways or tourists, my grandmother's grandmother told her that she couldn't go near the Gulf at night. Any kids who went down to the Gulf at night were taken by the Jetty Men, creatures half-man and half-fish who lived among the rocks and the sandbars and took the young and the weak away with them under the waves. My grandmother told me that story when I was little. She told it to us again when I was pregnant, the only time that Jake and I ever visited her.

I close my eyes and watch the old man and my son build the castle. He puts his hand on my son's shoulder. A black-veined webbing, papery and translucent, stretches out between the man's fingers and toes. Scales begin to show through his blue skin. His gills flutter behind his ears and he glances at me with an eye that has turned black and glassy. Then he picks up my son and walks into the Gulf, right through the tiny waves and under the hard green surface like he is part of the water and the water is part of him.

In that world, the world on the back of my eyelids, my son is somewhere under the Gulf with the Jetty Men, suspended below the surface in the salt where the sun comes shimmering green and warm across the bottom. Down where next week is never going to come. In that world, Jake and I watch passively from our folding chairs as our son vanishes forever, and Jake looks at me and grins and says *Hey, problem solved.* Then he grabs a beer for the road and walks out of my life.

I open my eyes. The old man is smiling at me again with human eyes.

"That old man looks just like a fish," Jake says.

My son has the corkscrew part of the Swiss Army knife out and he's drilling holes in the turrets.

"Do you remember–" Jake says.

"Yes."

He's on his hands and knees, looking for pieces of driftwood to use for cannons.

"When we were at your grandmother's house."

"I remember."

The Gulf rolls behind him.

# FRAGILE

Oh, but hold her, hold her like she's ten again, while she's crying the little dewdrop tears that mean *I have a dead uncle* instead of the torrent of *I have a dead lover* and you'll know the aching love of fatherhood, the devastating satisfaction of The Right Thing.

Because in your arms like this she's the quivering, fragile body that came to you for protection after so many jellyfish stings and scary movies, and you can't even remember the woman she's become, or the nights when you lay in bed beside your wife and listened to her through the Bible-page thin wall behind the headboard. Listened on the nights that she had friends over and they all sat cross-legged on her bed while she detailed to them how his cock curved up like Gonzo's nose inverted, or how she can only come when she sits on his face. And when your wife tells you that your daughter is in college and twenty-one years old and that's what they do in college, that's what you did in college, all you want to do is run to the next room and win her back with a pair of rollerskates or a Teddy Ruxpin or something that she used to love, but instead you just hit the remote and turn Conan up so that his voice is louder than theirs.

Then one Sunday afternoon while she's away again at school you find yourself in her room, looking for something that you forgot you were looking for, and you find in the corner of her closet beneath a blanket with stars on it a pink shoe-box that seems too small for shoes. Inside it you find her notes, all the notes that they passed palm-to-palm in hallways lined with green lockers and under desks studded with gum. They all read basically the same: *What's up?*
*Not much here just chillin' in Mrs. Smiths class. Can't wait til 3:00! What are you doing this afternoon? I have soccer. I can't wait til the dance. Okay gtg, ttyl.* And you smile and smell the yellowing paper and remember her coming home in seventh grade and how she must have felt the notes pressed against her skin inside her pocket, her secrets from the world.

Beneath all these notes there's a few more, letters in envelopes this time, with just her first name written on the outside. You look back at the door before you open the letter and you don't know why since your wife is off at yoga and you're alone in the quiet house. But you open the letter and read it and feel your stomach drop because it's everything you knew and didn't want to know; all the denying that your baby is a woman crashes and burns under lines of ink.

His name is at the bottom. You look again, and the handwriting does seem awful familiar, and there's his name, and it doesn't matter that it's only his first name; you know it's him as well as if he'd tagged it with the last name that you share.

And how can you even begin to wrap your mind around it? Yeah, she's a woman now, a strange woman who dresses in black and talks about modern art and the evils of capitalism and covers her walls with posters of bands you've never heard of and movies you've never seen. And then he's, yeah, he's younger, he was probably a mistake of your mother's and he's closer to her age than to your own.

There's pictures. One of him lying on his back in his bed with his shirt off, grinning stupidly at the camera, at whoever's holding the camera. Then there's another one, of the two of them in Florida, of your brother and your daughter kissing open-mouthed in front of Epcot Center. And at the very bottom of the box, smudged with fingerprints, another letter, folded and refolded so many times that it's coming apart at the creases, and you hold it lightly between your fingers and read in his handwriting everything that he says he's going to do to her next time they're together, and inside of you there's a welling of disgust and love, fury and jealousy. You fold the letter and put it back in the box and put all the letters on top of it and set the box in the corner again under the star-flecked blanket.

Back in your own room, you find the box beneath your bed and unlock it and take out the gun that your wife made you buy fifteen years ago when there was a murder two blocks away and it's your job to keep your family safe. You wonder what you're going to do with the thing and whether it will fire even if you want it to, and you put it in your pocket and go to the car. Outside it looks exactly like Sunday afternoon, golden and slow.

So you drive the four blocks to his apartment and knock on the green door. He opens it and looks surprised to see you. He's in his sweat pants and an undershirt like he's just woken up. He lets you in and offers you some pot, but the thought of putting your mouth on the bong where his has been, and where his mouth has been, is too much and you just say, "No, thanks."

Sitting on the couch and looking at him while he stands there fiddling with the bong and a tin box that used to hold a watch and now holds weed, he looks like a kid – he looks like you did twenty years ago, but taller. He looks like your brother again and you think that maybe you'll be okay, maybe you can just forget it or warn him or they'll get over it on their own. "Everything okay?" he says.

"Yeah."

"You sure?" he says, flicking the lighter at the bong. And then he asks, he *asks* about her. "Jill okay?" And you look at him and tell him that she's yours, she's your daughter, and that you know.

He drops the bong and starts to say things about how it was the drugs and how he never thought it would go that far and how he was fucked up and needed help and didn't mean anything and he was so sorry, and then he says that he loves her, and you don't even know that the gun is in your hand until you see him backing away, his face ashen. Then he says that it wasn't his fault and that hey, *she* came onto *him*, and you don't even know you've pulled the trigger until his face explodes.

Then he's not your brother anymore, he's not anyone anymore; he's a twitching heap on the floor of this apartment that's smaller than your garage. It's not your brother bubbling and gurgling his last couple of breaths. Your brother died a long time ago. This was someone who threatened, and you had to protect. And then you realize that you can't protect if you're in jail, and you don't have a boat to take him wrapped in plastic and chains out into the ocean to drop him to the bottom with the sand and the lobsters. You don't have a plastic-lined slaughterhouse with a whirring bandsaw to turn him into pig food. So you break the window and you take his television and his DVD player and his laptop and his iPod and the weed and his wallet and all the other money that you can find and get back in your car. You drive to the supermarket seven miles up the road and throw it all in a dumpster in the back. Then you go home and wait for the cops to come. A few days later, when your wife is off at her ridiculous yoga class and your daughter is in town for the weekend, the cops come.

So you talk to them and look surprised and sad and concerned while your daughter tries to read your face, and finally the cops leave. You tell her that it was a robbery, and she knows how he was, he probably tried to stop them. And you watch your daughter's face: an instant of confusion, then disbelief, then the fall of her eyebrows and jaw as it hits her and the hurt, the hurt. Then you can see her remember that he was not supposed to be the love of her life but a man who came over to dinner once a month, so she tightens the corners of her mouth and blinks back tears and says, "Oh, no."

Then you feel yourself starting to cry, too. You open your arms and she collapses into them and cries for him while you cry for everything and everyone who ever had to be the protector, who had to endure the savage and the carnal and the wicked all for the smallest bit of love, and you hold her like she's a little girl because she is, she is for an instant your little girl again, and you smile and feel her heart against your chest and realize that you're kissing her a little longer and harder than you really ought to.

The wind slipped around the walls and coated the treestand in cold. Inside, Max and Tommy–brothers, eleven and fourteen– looked out over the clearing. Tommy lit a cigarette and leaned back against the wet wooden wall. He inhaled slowly with his eyes closed, let the smoke drift lazily out of his nostrils. Max thought he looked just like Robert used to. Robert, their oldest brother, his absence keeping him in the forefront of Max's mind more than he had ever been when he was alive.

"Won't the smoke scare the deer away?" Max said.

"You'll scare the deer away if you don't shut up," Tommy whispered back. He opened his eyes. He looked out over the field. The dusk was pooling around the trees as the sun sank to the west. The clearing was fifty yards across, nothing but tall grass and scrub brush between the stand and the feeder at the far side, the feeder that spilled corn into a neat yellow pile in the dirt. Far past the trees, just at the edge of sight, the Mississippi river ran swift and quiet.

Max folded his hands on the wall of the treestand and rested his chin on top of them. He looked down at the ground ten feet below. A squirrel skittered around the base.

"We're downwind of the feeder," Tommy whispered, his eyes still closed. "Deer can't smell the smoke from here anyway." He took another long drag.

Max didn't know where Tommy had gotten the cigarettes. He was older than Max, but still too young to buy them. This was November 1947, time when the War was just beginning to become a memory instead of a fact of life.

Tommy snubbed the cigarette out on the wall and tapped Max between the shoulder blades. He leaned his head close to Max's ear and whispered, barely above a breath, "There." Max smelled the smoke in his voice. Tommy pointed and Max followed his finger out into the field, out into the tall grass where the shadows were growing longer. At the edge of the clearing, a doe padded across the grass, slow and graceful and silent. She blended and disappeared as the breeze came in and the grass swayed in the cold.

"Should I shoot her now?" Max said.

"Not yet," Tommy said. "Wait til she gets to the feeder."

Max picked the 30-30 up off the floor and braced it on the edge of the stand. He looked along the iron sights, felt the hard wooden butt of the gun molding into his shoulder. He held the gun the way Robert did, the way Robert had taught Tommy and Tommy had showed him, as the deer tiptoed towards the feeder.

You're never going to hit anything if you don't feel comfortable with the gun, Robert says. He picks the 30-30 up with one hand, swings the lever, ejects the empty shell. He says, Gun should be part of you, like an extension of your body. He puts the gun to his shoulder and aims at the paper target on the tree, fifty feet away. His tongue comes out of his mouth slightly and his finger moves slowly and the gunshot cracks across the morning air. The bullet slams into the tree an inch outside of the bullseye.

Max sits on a stump and watches them. Robert hands the gun to Tommy. It seems long and awkward in his hands. Tommy fumbles with the lever until the shell comes out. Then he hefts the gun and fires in a single motion. The bullet is lost in the woods.

Got to have patience, Robert says.

Can I try? Max says.

Still too young, buddy. Dad'll be pissed if he finds out I let you shoot. He sits down on the stump next to Max and puts his elbow on top of Max's head. Max squirms while Robert slouches against him. Robert says, You make a good armrest, you know that?

Max laughs.

I'll teach you in a couple of years, Robert says. He lights a cigarette and closes his eyes and takes a long drag. Tommy throws the gun to the ground, exasperated.

How many times I got to say patience? Robert says, without opening his eyes.

Tommy sits down in the dirt. The wind whispers in the trees as the sun brightens the blue in the sky. The air smells cold and fresh.

Max watched the deer through the iron sights. It was almost dark. It was getting hard to see her. She stopped at the

18

feeder, looked around, her ears twitching. Then she bent down to eat. Tommy's finger slid slowly into a thumbs up.

Max pressed the safety and it switched over with a faint click. The doe jerked her head up, stared straight into the stand. Max pulled the trigger and the woods rocked with the reverberation of the gunshot. He smelled the sulfurous gunpowder smell and felt the faint heat on the barrel and watched the deer careen away into the woods.

"Shit yeah!" Tommy yelled, slapping Max on the back. "You see her jump? You see her? You nailed her!"

"I didn't see," Max said, scanning the edge of the clearing.

"Nailed her! Let's go, she can't have got far."

The climbed out of the treestand and jogged across the clearing while the cold came in with the shadows. The pile of corn beside the feeder was tumped over, kernels scattered. Behind the feeder a bubblegum-pink spot of frothy blood showed in the waning light.

"See that?" Tommy said, pointing at the blood, "See how it's all pink? That's from the oxygen. You must've got her in the lung." He walked to the edge of the clearing where the deer had disappeared. "Here you go," he said. He took out his flashlight and shined it on a leaf. A tiny droplet of reddish-black blood stained the green.

Max followed Tommy into the woods. The trees were dark and the undergrowth was thick; the vines tore at Max's hands as he made his way through. Tommy shined the light at the ground and the trees. He crept in a zigzag away from the clearing, following the path of the deer. The clues were minuscule but glaring–a broken branch here, another spot of blood here. A pink puddle where the deer had fallen down. And finally the deer, tan and tiny in the dark woods, collapsed behind a log with its head at a funny angle, a red spot of fur on its side where the bullet went in.

Max held its front legs and Tommy held the back as they carried it back to the cabin. The cabin would be warm, with light and fire and food. They hurried. The wind came out of the north and blanketed them with cold.

Robert stirs the beans in the pot over the fire. Tommy struggles to clean the 30-30. Max adjusts the radio.

19

Turn the radio off, Robert says.

Max turns the radio off. Tommy fits a piece of gauze on the end of a slender metal rod and dips it in solvent and slides it down the barrel of the gun. It comes out black. He puts a new piece of gauze on and does it again, the metal brushing metal with a singing sliding sound.

Wind's picking up out there, Robert says.

Max says, Good thing we got the fire.

Yeah, good thing, we'll be warm in here. Robert puts the spoon in the beans and tastes them. Then he says, You hear that wind?

Max and Tommy listen.

It's not just wind, Robert says. You can hear things in it.

Outside, the wind whips around the trees, whistles along the edges of the house. A tree groans near the cabin. A branch snaps off and crashes to the forest floor, somewhere far away.

Robert says, You guys know about the Wendigo?

The boys shake their heads. Robert slides the screen in front of the fireplace and the room gets dark and shadowy. He wants it to be scary. It *is* scary.

Dad told me about it, Robert says. So I can tell you about it, now that you're old enough to hear it and I'm old enough to tell it. So you hear that wind out there?

Nods.

There's voices in that wind, if you listen hard enough. Whispers, screams.

He pauses. The wind rattles the windows. There's a wailing sound, far away. Robert's face is a smattering of orange and black in the crackling firelight.

Robert says, These are the voices of the people taken by the Wendigo. Wendigo lives out there, out in the woods. It's a spirit, a dark spirit, that lives and breathes in everything that's dark in the woods. It drives people crazy, mad.

Max pulls his knees to his chest. Tommy starts putting the gun back together.

Robert says, People go out in the woods, at night, and they start to lose it, start to lose it when the Wendigo is coming for them. They go crazy, and sometimes they kill each other, eat each other, because the Wendigo makes them think that eating the people they kill will make them stronger. But sometimes, the Wendigo takes them away itself. The people go mad, and they run out into the night, screaming and crying, and the Wendigo swoops down. It grabs them and flies with them close to the ground until they are going so fast that the person catches fire and burns up and becomes part of the wind.

He is quiet. The trees bend and pop outside.

In the morning, Robert continues, there's nothing left of them, just footprints, getting farther and farther apart. And a voice in the wind.

The wind comes through the cracks in the walls. Max shivers. He says, It's getting cold.

Robert says, That's how it starts.

This is December of 1942. This is the last time the three of them are together in the cabin. It's two weekends before Robert gets on the bus and heads away to the big war.

Tommy tied the deer's feet together and hung it upside down from a tree. "I'll show you how to clean her," he said.

The lights from the cabin made the deer barely visible in the night. Tommy drew a small, thin knife with a silver blade that reflected the moon. He pressed the blade into the deer near its groin and drew it straight and slow all the way down to its neck. A line of blood followed the blade and steam wisped its way out of the body and into the black.

"She'll go bad if you leave her guts in her," Tommy said. He reached his hands inside the deer and pulled out a bunch of brown and red and black stuff. Then he walked over to Max, his hands black with blood, and ran his thumbs under Max's eyes, painting him like an Indian brave. "Your first deer," he said. "When I got my first one, Robert did it to me. And he said Dad did it to him." He wiped the rest of the blood off on the front of his jeans. "Wait 'til we tell dad," he said. "Your first trip out without him or Robert, and you get your first deer."

Max felt the blood drying on his cheekbones. He smelled the warm and meaty copper smell. The smell made him think of death, of the dead.

"You're a hunter now," Tommy said.

Max and Tommy are listening to the radio in the living room when the car pulls up outside. A military man–an officer in a uniform–and a preacher in black with a white collar get out and talk to each other, point at the house.

Oh shit, Tommy says. Oh shit.

Max and Tommy stare at the radio while the men approach in the corners of their eyes. The doorbell rings. They hear their mother trot down the stairs, the door open, and then her screaming. She screams, NonononononoNONO*NOOO!* and she runs back upstairs. Her bedroom door slams shut. Her closet door slams shut. She's still yelling No up there.

The men whisper to each other in the doorway before they come into the living room.

How you doing boys? the officer says.

Tommy gets up off the couch and turns off the radio. He goes into the kitchen. A minute later Max follows him, and the two men look at each other and head into the kitchen.

Tommy says, You guys want some Cokes or something?

I'll take a Coke, the officer says.

Sure, the preacher says, Matter of fact, lets all sit down and have some Cokes.

They all sit down at the table with their Cokes. Upstairs the door rattles as their mother bangs her heels against it. She's screaming into a coat.

The men drink their Cokes and try to think of what to say. The boys stare at them.

Tommy says, Is Robert dead?

The men look at each other and back at the boys. The preacher sets his Bible on the table and puts his hand around Tommy's on the Coke bottle. The preacher says, Yes, I'm sorry.

Max starts to cry. Tommy scrunches his lips and his eyes together.

It's okay to cry, boys, the Preacher says.

They cry for a minute as the preacher holds their hands against the wet cold glass of the Coke bottles. The officer stares out the window, taps his finger on the table. He finishes his Coke. The mother has become silent upstairs.

Tommy looks at the table. He says, How did it happen?

22

The preacher looks at the officer. The officer leans forward and says, I got a letter from his commanding officer. Private Buchanan was uncommonly brave.

How did it happen? Tommy says. Max puts the heels of his palms against his eyes.

The officer takes a breath. They were outside Paris, he says, charging hard. He was with one of Patton's divisions. They came under some artillery–

The preacher says, You sure you should be telling them this?

I want to know, Tommy says.

The officer says, A shell landed practically right on top of him. There wasn't much left. Didn't even find the dog tags.

This is too much for them, the preacher says. They're kids.

Tommy says, We're not kids.

Yes you are.

No we're not.

Hmm, the preacher says. He sits back and drinks his Coke.

Tommy says, Where is he?

He's with God, the preacher says.

Where's his body?

The officer shrugs. He says, Gone, kid. Blammo.

Well that's definitely inappropriate, the preacher says.

Whatever.

Max sits with his arms crossed. His eyes are wet and raw. Tommy scratches his head. He says, So how can you be sure he's dead?

The officer leans in and says, Trust me, kid.

Then their mother is standing in the doorway. She's wearing a blue dress that's wrinkled all up the front. Her hair is loose and wild. Her eyes are red-rimmed. She clasps her hands in front of her and says, I'm ready now.

Then there are confusing days, with people coming and going and talks from their mother and talks from their father. There is a funeral with a coffin with nothing inside. Then life returns.

Until Tommy sneaks into Max's room one night three weeks later. Wake up, Max, he says. He shakes him on the shoulder. Max groans awake.

What, he says.

Tommy's eyes are wide and liquid bright. He says, Robert is alive!

What are you talking about?

He's alive! The shell missed him, he ducked at the last minute. I got a letter from him, he told me all about it. That's why they don't have a body, he's still alive. He's coming home, too. He's trying to find a boat. Once he finds a boat, he's coming home.

What?

You'll see.

Then he leaves and Max watches the moon coast across the sky outside his window.

The deer hung from the tree, gutted, swaying in the wind, its eyes black glassy beads.

Inside the cabin, Tommy cooked beans over the fireplace. He instructed Max on how to clean the gun. "Unscrew the barrel," he said. "Dip the gauze in the solvent, run it through, then throw it away. You're done when it comes out clean."

"How long does that take?"

"A while. Probably a dozen pieces."

Tommy spooned some beans into a bowl and placed it steaming on the floor in front of Max. He served himself and sat down at the table. He turned the radio on and adjusted it until he found the football game. He leaned over his bowl, eating quickly, his eyes black, darting around the room.

They ate their beans and listened. The wind wrapped itself around the cabin.

Tommy comes into Max's room three more times, a few weeks apart. He raves about the letters. He curses the lack of a boat.

In the days he is restless. He shakes and his eyes look distant and dark. He wanders off into the woods for hours, then comes back like nothing is wrong. Says he was exploring. He's strange in the day. He's crazy at night.

He wakes up in a sweat one night, screaming. His parents run into the room. Max can hear him screaming. He hears thrashing in the bed, his parents holding him down. Tommy is screaming Get on the boat, Robert! You're going to miss the boat!

The fire burned down to coals that glowed like demons' eyes in the fireplace. The boys lay down in their cots, side by side. The gun leaned reassembled and clean in the corner. The air was heavy with solvent and baked beans.

The fire sent shadows playing on the walls, and cold seeped in under the door, coating the floor like a layer of liquid ice. Tommy's fingers drummed on the side of his cot.

"You hear that wind?" he whispered.

Max listened. The wind coursed through the woods and made everything moan with a terrible life.

"It's really blowing," Tommy said. "It might storm."

"I'm glad we're inside," Max said.

They were silent. Max closed his eyes and felt himself drifting off. The coals shifted in the fireplace with a muffled crunch.

"Mom and dad think I'm crazy," Tommy said.

"What?"

"I've heard them talking," he said. "Because of Robert. They think I'm crazy. I'm not crazy." He turned over in his cot and faced Max. "You don't think I'm crazy, do you?"

Max shrugged. Tommy rolled over. He tossed in his bed. Threw his covers to the floor. He lay tense and quiet for a few minutes. Then he sat up.

"Robert's not dead," Tommy said.

"Tommy—"

"Why do you think there's no body?"

"He's dead, Tommy."

Tommy sat on the edge of the cot, the tips of his toes barely scraping the floor. The fire burned in little red circles in the back of his eyes. His nose and his lips twitched. His hands gripped tight on the cot's metal frame.

Max put his hand on Tommy's knee. "Tommy. Robert is dead."

"He's not!" Tommy said. He got out of bed. "He's been sending me letters. Where are these letters coming from?"

25

"Tommy, you don't have any letters. No one else has seen them."

"You think I'm just going to show those letters to anyone? I'm not crazy! They'll go over there if they see those letters they'll go over there and find him and make him fight again. Then he *will* die! He'll die for sure!"

"They can't make him fight anymore. The war's over."

Tommy pulled his shirt off and stretched it over his head. He grunted and threw it to the floor and stomped down on a sleeve, tugged hard on the other one. It ripped, but didn't break, so he threw it into the fire. It sizzled and flared at the edges before bursting into a bright orange tongue of flame. Tommy's eyes were wild in the firelight.

Outside, the wind howled. The door shook on its hinges.

"He's alive! He's been living with a beautiful French woman! Why do you think there's no body? He caught the artillery shell and threw it back and ran off and he's goddammit he's alive!"

"Stop it, Tommy!" Max said. He sat up in bed and pulled the covers tight around him.

"Don't you tell me to stop you telling me to stop? You don't want him back?"

"Of course I want him back."

"Then we've just got to help him find the boat! He's waiting on the boat and he's going to miss it and be stuck in France and have to fight forever. He's probably out there waiting right now. We can't let him miss it."

He opened the door and the cold rushed like a tide through the room. Outside, flurries of tiny snowflakes blew sideways through the black trees. The deer bobbed and rocked, its empty insides red in the faint moonlight. "Robert!" Tommy yelled into the blackness. "Hey Robert!"

"Come inside!" Max yelled over the wind.

"Robert! The boat!"

"Shut the door, Tommy!"

Tommy looked back into the room. His teeth shone moonlight white while the fire reflected in his eyes. Then he ran barefoot and shirtless into the night.

Max ran to the door. Outside, the night was thick, black. The snow blew onto his skin and melted and left him soggy and cold. In the distance, over the howling of the wind, Tommy was yelling, yelling about Robert, yelling about the boat. Max ran in the direction of his voice. He followed the trail that led towards the treestand, sprinting in the cold. He stopped to catch his breath. He heard Tommy yelling off in the woods to his left. The words were mangled by the wind, but he heard him say, "The boat! There it is!" and then nothing else. Just the wind wild and fierce in the trees.

He walked through the woods by the light of the pale setting moon. After a couple of minutes, the ground became wet and squishy. He saw the river deep and black and impossibly wide in front of him. He stumbled down the hill toward the water and walked along the dark bank. After a while, he found a footprint, right on the water's edge, his brother's bare footprint. The prints came from the woods, down the hill, far apart in his bounding leaping flight.

"Tommy?" he said. The wind ripped the top of the black water into a mist and carried his voice away into the night.

He reached down and put his hand in the water; the cold stung his fingertips. He walked downriver, looking out at the water. He couldn't see the other side or the bottom. It was like looking into flowing emptiness. He climbed the hill and walked back to the cabin. The cold swallowed up the moon and the darkness fell like a black blanket across the woods. He walked past the deer when he came out of the forest. The deer watched him with a blank dead eye.

The fire was burned out inside the cabin. Max poked at it, tried to stir it back into flame; it was nothing but dead ash. The cold seeped in through the walls and made him shiver. He took a blanket off the bed and wrapped it around him. He picked up the 30-30 and loaded it, then he crouched down in the corner opposite the door, his knees tucked in and the blanket around him and the gun tight against his chest. The wind screamed outside all night long as Max stared at the blackness outside the window.

His knees were sore and his eyes heavy by the time the square of sky in the window began to lighten. Max watched it change from black to gray to blue; the wind died down and daytime animals started making noise, and finally he heard his father's pickup rumbling up the road. He heard the engine turn off, the car door open and shut, and then footsteps on the gravel. His father opened the door and stared at him, silent, and then took him in his arms.

Then there were hazy days. Search crews, teams of people walking side by side through the woods, calling Tommy's name. Bloodhounds snuffling along the river bank. Boats trolling the brown water. And questions. *Where did he go? What did he say to you?*

And Max couldn't think of anything to say except for, "He went to find Robert."

Then there were more of those talks, gentle, soothing monologues from adults, like the ones he'd heard when Robert died, and then there was another empty coffin, lowered into the ground beside Robert's.

And then he was expected to live the rest of his life.


Max Buchanan stands on the shore of the Gulf of Mexico, where he built his house, as far as possible from the cabin in the hills. The cold wind is blowing in from the land. It speaks to him. It tells him of its flight, when it howled out of Canada and across the plains, past the cows in the Dakotas that lean their hot heavy hides together for warmth. When it bent and shivered the late-harvest corn in Nebraska and startled the ducks in the ponds in Arkansas, who shook the water from their wings and took to whistling flight. The wind whispers about northern Mississippi, where the river runs fast and brown and wild, a place where a doe puts her nose to the wind, pricks her ears, and bounds past an empty cabin and into the dark woods in a flash of whitetail and speed.

Max is old now. His joints pop as he pulls his jacket tight around him. Max hates this wind. To him, it is nothing but cold, a hard, hungering cold that swallows up everything that's good about the outdoors–the blue in the air, the crispness in the leaves–until nothing is left but still gray sky. He hates the wind, the voices he hears in it, and he's spent his entire life trying to get away from it.

But even as he stands on the green frothing edge of the continent, the wind hits him and chills him through his bones.

Max trots up the beach to his house and shuts the door behind him. He sits down inside and turns the TV up. The wind is loud outside. It deadens the crashing of the waves and the rustling of the sea oats. It sings with all its voices, whispers stories that no one else knows.

Night comes and Max turns the TV off and listens. He turns out the lights in the house and climbs into bed. He stares at the door on the other side of the room and trembles.

The wind moves the things around the beach house. It silences the Gulf and swallows the summer up with its hungering cold. It murmurs and chuckles beneath the windows.

Max watches the door. The wind slips under it like the whispers of a ghost.

## THINGS YOU CAN DO WITH A CAN OF CAMPBELL'S SOUP

You can pour the soup into a pot. Cook it. Eat it. Recycle it.

Clean it out and peel the label off and take it to your Cub Scout troop meeting. Take a hammer and nail and hammer holes into the sides until you've made the shape of something festive for Christmas. Or you can write *fart* or *boobs*. Then stick a tea candle in the bottom and paint the walls with holiday cheer or profanity. Compare your lantern to those of your Cub Scout friends, the friends you won't talk to again after high school.

You can catch fireflies in it. You'll have to cover the top so that they won't escape, but then their light won't get out.

Take several cans and line them up on a sawhorse and walk three hundred yards across a field under the summer sun to where you left your dad's rifle. Do this early in the afternoon when there's no chance he'll come home from work. Lie on your belly in the grass. Feel the butt of the gun firm against your shoulder. Breathe slowly, quiet; listen to the insects whirring near your ears. Hold your breath while you squeeze the trigger. The report will be loud. Don't be startled. Watch through the scope as the can flips into the dirt. Feel powerful.

Gather a bunch for a high school club and donate them to the homeless shelter.

You can paint a picture of it and call it art. It's been done before.

You can mix some half-and-half and some seasonings and vegetables and diced-up chicken into a few cans of tomato soup and say it's a centuries-old family recipe for tomato bisque. Serve it to your girlfriend while you sit naked on the couch together. She'll be impressed. She'll become your wife.

Make an ugly flower pot out of it and give it to her as an anniversary present.

Feed it to your kids when the rain's trickling down the windows and your wife is working and you are feeling very lazy. And you are out of peanut butter and jelly.

You can eat it yourself when your wife tells you you're not worth cooking for.

Hold it in your hand at the supermarket and marvel at its simplicity. It is metal; everything else is plastic and fluorescent and space-aged and extreme, but the can of Campbell's soup looks exactly the same as the one that your grandfather bought during the Depression. Back when he scrounged for pennies by selling coal that bounced out of the train, back when he bought the soup from a man who is now dead.

You can fill it with things. Marbles. Seashells. Water that's dripped from the soggy spot in the roof of the living room, the spot you never got around to fixing.

The can can hold all that. Hold it in your hand and look at the shelf. So many choices. Chicken noodle that smells like the flu. Vegetable beef that pops and sizzles over a campfire. Tomato that you can't bring yourself to buy anymore.

Take a can off the shelf. The can has heft. Fill it with yourself. You can fit the things in it that you can't fit anywhere else, the loss and the jealousy and the rage. If you want it bad enough, it can hold your children, wherever they are, and your parents, if they were alive, and the friends and the parties and everything else that you had before you started coming home to an empty apartment and eating Campbell's soup for dinner every night. Toss the can a couple times in your hand like a pitcher biding his time at the mound. Wind up and chuck it as hard as you can down the aisle and leave a Bean-with-Bacon-shaped dent in the side of that woman's head, the woman that looks kind of like your ex-wife. People will see you. They'll come after you. That's okay. You have an entire shelf of red and white ammo. You can knock them down, knock them down, bring them all down around you while you laugh and throw and throw. Feel powerful again.

You can hook two cans together with a piece of string and try to have a conversation with someone who isn't very far away. Go ahead and put the can right up to your ear. All you'll hear is metal and string.

# HOLIDAY

The storm clouds slid by fat and heavy. From way out over the gulf, the wind blew in and tumbled the water into brown, low waves that sloughed their way to shore. The umbrella guy pulled the umbrellas out of the sand and folded them up and put them away in the hut near the road while the wind got colder. Taylor watched him for a minute, then went back to watching his wife. Haley was swimming close to shore, diving under the waves and doing handstands in the dirty surf. Her hair was slicked back dark and close down her back, and with her tiny nose and her black eyes, she reminded Taylor of a sea otter. He pressed the heels of his hands into his eyes.

She came out of the water with her arms wrapped around her, her teeth bit into her lower lip. "It's cold," she said. She had bits of seaweed stuck all over her.

"It's going to storm," Taylor said.

"It was nice out there though. It was warm."

"Sharks come out when the water gets like this."

"They do not."

"They do so. When the water gets all churned up, they get confused, come in close to shore and bite people."

"Come on," she said. She pushed him on the shoulder. Taylor looked at the sand. Haley hugged her knees close to her chest. "What do you want to do now?" she said.

"I don't know."

"If it storms we could go see a movie."

"We can see a movie at home."

"But I don't know what else to do if it's raining."

"We didn't come here to see movies. We're supposed to be getting away. You know, recuperating." He started burying his feet. He piled sand on top of them until it looked like his calves just disappeared into a big pile of sugar. "It might not even rain," he said.

"Umbrella guy's putting his stuff away. He probably knows better."

"I don't care what umbrella guy's doing."

"You don't have to be so angry at me all the time. It's not my fault."

"I'm not angry at you."

"I mean, I can't help it," Haley said. "And I'm upset, too."

"I don't want to talk about this right now."

"We don't have to."

The rain came across the gulf in a frothing white sheet. A fishing boat motored by at full speed just in front of it. The wind was cold and smelled of metal and wetness.

"Here it comes," Haley said.

They got up and ran toward the road. The rain chased them up the shore, patting into the sand and turning it brown and mottled.

"Our shirts," Haley said.

"We'll get them later."

There was a convenience store near the road. Two boys stood outside under the awning. They were barefoot and shirtless in wet cutoff jeans, silent and tan, eyes squinted from days in the sun. One of them sucked on a popsicle. They watched as Taylor and Haley limped across the parking lot, the rocky asphalt rough on their feet. The boy with the popsicle bit it with his teeth. His eyes were blue and cold.

Inside the store everything smelled of air conditioner and electricity. The fluorescent lights painted the walls chalky. The clerk, an old Indian woman, stood behind a thick piece of plexiglass. "You buying?" she said.

Taylor and Haley stood panting and dripping on the white tile. "Buying?" Taylor said.

"You buy or you get out."

"Okay," he said.

"We should get some beer," Haley said.

"You want beer?"

"I can drink as much as I want now."

"I guess so."

They paid for a six pack and stood next to the magazine rack, looking out the window. Haley flipped through the magazines. She took a beer from the pack and tried to open it. She handed it to Taylor, squeezed her fingers in her other fist.

"It hurts my hands," she said.

Taylor twisted the lid off and handed it back to her.

The rain started to let up and the two boys walked around the corner and came back with a couple of old bicycles. One punched the other in the arm. They laughed. Then they got on the bikes and rode slowly away. The sun broke out from behind the clouds.

Back on the beach, Taylor pulled his shirt out of the mud. It was wet and sandy. He shook it out and sat down on it and opened a beer. Haley sat down beside him. Near the road, umbrella guy was unlocking the hut.

"You think you might want to go swimming with me?" Haley said.

"Not really." He pushed the beer into the sand and picked it back up, a ring of brownish white sand caked around the bottom.

"It wasn't supposed to storm every day," she said.

"You can't control the weather."

"I know. I just wanted you to have a good time. I wanted you to be happy again."

"I'm happy."

"Happy like you were before."

Her voice was creaky. Without looking at her, Taylor could tell she was doing the face, the one where she scrunched everything up like a mouse and tried not to cry. He used to think it was cute.

"We're going to be okay," she said. "We're going to be okay, right?"

Taylor drew lines in the sand.

"I mean, we can maybe even try again."

"There's no point."

"Maybe though. I mean, we can pray–"

"Praying's not going to do it, Haley."

"Well we shouldn't–" She stopped talking. Looked out over the water. Things were moving around offshore, making ripples on the surface.

"The doctor says you can't carry it to term. That's all there is to it."

"It might change."

"It won't. And I'm not going through that again." He stood up and walked toward the water. The waves slid up the shore and covered his feet like foamy beer. They went out again and took his footprints with them and left dozens of blue and silver and pink coquinas ooching their spiral path back into the sand. Haley stood behind him.

"Well, there's other things we can do."

"I'm really not interested."

"Or it can be just us."

"That's just not how I wanted it."

"It's not how I wanted it, either."

The warm wind that was left over from the storm blew her hair out to the side. The tears were wet on her face.

"Please please don't be like this," Haley said.

"I'm not being like this."

"You are."

Taylor waded into the water. Tiny fish nipped at his heels.

"We'll figure it out," she said.

"I don't know."

"We will. We can."

Umbrella guy stabbed an umbrella into the sand. He opened it in a flash of pink and blue. He walked back to the hut and walked along the beach with another one over his shoulder. Taylor watched him and then looked out over the gulf and then back at Haley.

"I just don't think I love you enough," he said.

She sat down in the sand. She drank her beer.

"I'm going to go for a swim," Taylor said. He waded out until the water was over his head. The wind was calming down and the gulf was nearly flat. He dove under and opened his eyes and swam to the bottom where the water was dark and cold.

# PEOPLE I'LL NEVER SEE AGAIN

My dad was pissing into the snow at the far end of the parking lot. I stood as far away from him as I could and still keep him happy. He said he was going to teach me the true story of the Continental Divide. The snow was blowing in sideways from the high mountains. I kept my hands in my pockets. My face was cold.

He was trying to write his name in the snow. He was up to C-H-R, but Christopher is a long name to write in piss, so he stopped. He shook himself and turned to me and grinned.

"All right, now follow me," he said. "I'm going to show you something they don't teach you in seventh grade. Won't teach you in school at all, for that matter."

He zipped up and tromped across the parking lot. I trailed along behind him. His feet crunched in the snow and left dirty waffle-iron footprints.

"Now that piss over there," he said, jerking his thumb back at the end of the parking lot, "that piss is going to end up in the Atlantic Ocean. All the water that falls on that side of the Divide, on the East side, ends up in rivers that feed into the Mississippi, and that goes down into the Gulf and into the Atlantic."

He kept looking back over his shoulder at me while he talked. I looked at my feet. People were milling about between their cars and the visitor center. Mom was sitting in the car with the heater on. There was a big iron sign in the middle of the parking lot that said *Welcome to the Center of the Country* in giant letters with other stuff in smaller letters below it. It probably said everything you could want to know about the Continental Divide, but we walked right past it. At the other end of the parking lot, he unzipped his pants and picked right back up with the I of Christopher.

"You gotta pee?"

I shook my head.

"Eh. Well. This piss here," he said, hefting the arc of piss for emphasis, "is going to end up in the Pacific. Just think, all those surfers and stuff in California won't see it coming."

A little girl said something and pointed; her mother covered her eyes and hurried her toward the visitor center. Some college kids had their cameras out; they were taking pictures, giggling and skirting the outside of the lot, looking for the best view.

My dad laughed as the stream petered out halfway through the S. "Tide's rising in San Francisco! Tell them boys at Alcatraz, now's their chance! Make a break for it!"

"Dad," I said, pushing the snow around with my foot, "people are watching."

"So what." His face was red from the wind. "We'll never see any of these people again."

We got back in the car.

"Everything come out okay?" my mom said, and she and my dad both cracked up. I leaned my head against the window and closed my eyes.

We backed out of the parking lot and started down the mountain. The snow was picking up, weighing on the windshield wipers. My dad opened the window a crack and some snow shot back into my face. I moved to the other side. He sat up real straight in his seat and spit thick black tobacco spit out the window onto the pavement. We were driving slow and cars were piling up behind us.

"I taught our boy all about the Continental Divide," my dad said.

"Did you, now?" my mom said.

"He didn't know the physics of it. Fascinating stuff, when you think about it."

We passed a sign that read *Overlook Ahead 500ft.* We came around the corner and saw another big iron sign with an area to pull off the road and look at something.

"We'll overlook that overlook," my mom said. Another explosion of laughter from the front seats. I pulled my hat down tighter over my head.

"But it's pretty profound, if you really think about it." My dad was getting philosophical. He did this sometimes. "Me, I'm just one man, but now there's part of me everywhere. Going to flow all over the country, out into both oceans. Hell, maybe some of it end up in Japan, some of it in England. Maybe meet back up in Australia or something."

"You should have done it too," my mom said, looking back at me. "How often do you get an opportunity like that?"

37

"I told him to.  He was bladder shy.  Too many people around, he said."

"Oh honey," she said, reaching back, taking off my hat and smoothing my hair down, "you're never going to see any of those people again."

We came to a straight place on the road, and the first car behind us floored it to get by.  It was a big orange SUV.  There was a girl in the back seat; she looked a few years older than me, probably in high school already.  She looked right at me and smiled.  And I thought about never seeing those people again.

In that one electric second of eye contact I could see her life and mine, bright pulsing cords stretching out into the endless, twisting and writhing and never touching except for once, this one instant on the road in the snow in Colorado.  The cords touched tangentially in an explosion of light and fire, and then hers spun away from mine, unspooling endlessly into the black, infinitely far away while mine kept grinding on alongside my parents'.

Maybe we cross again.  Maybe I run over her cat in a neighborhood in Montana and walk door to door with the body until I find her for the tearful apology.  Maybe she sells me a ticket to a Broadway show in New York.  Or our eyes meet again, sixty years from now, across the deck of a dolphin tour boat in the Gulf in Florida while the seagulls squawk overhead.

Maybe I marry her.  Maybe I never see her again.

That girl would love to talk to me about this kind of thing.  My parents wouldn't.  My dad would find some way to turn the explosion of light and fire into a dirty joke.  My mom would ask me what tangential means.

The snow came in heavy through the crack in the window and soaked the seat beside me.  My dad leaned out to spit.  He had his hand on the shifter and my Mom's hand was on top of his.  Outside the window the trees creaked under the ice, the wind carried snow into the upper layers of the atmosphere and back, and beneath frozen surfaces, ancient creeks rushed my dad's piss in opposite directions to opposite oceans.

I pulled myself deeper into my jacket and watched the valleys slide past outside the window and thought, maybe that's as profound as life gets.

# AUDACIOUS

She was a pickpocket.

She haunted the subway station on 34<sup>th</sup> and Holloway, where every morning Gerald waited for his train on the same cold concrete bench. He watched her through thick glasses. She was young, frail and thin, waif-like, with short shaggy black hair, and she moved like a ghost, drifting in and out of sight as the crowd milled about.

She made him look forward to the mornings. She made him feel sparks. Watching her was the only time that Gerald had felt alive since the morning that he found Dolores–his wife of fifty three years–face down in her Cheerios on a Sunday morning, dead from a stroke.

Gerald's pickpocket wore black leggings covered by a short blue jean skirt. She wore two jackets, windbreaker over denim; lots of pockets, Gerald figured. Sometimes she wore sunglasses, even though she was underground.

She was good, crafty and swift and clever, and not greedy– you get caught when you get greedy. Gerald learned her patterns as he watched her on the way to work.

Not work, really. After Dolores died, and after the funeral and the family and the random visitors bringing potluck stuff over to mold in the fridge, he found himself alone in the house. He had been retired for nine years before she died, and they had never done much of anything. They never traveled or went to parties or joined any golf clubs. But they were in the house together, living close and separate lives side by side. She was there, a constant, a daily affirmation, like the soreness of his right rear molar or the ingrown toenail on his middle toe. A part of life.

Once she was gone, there was nothing there but an empty house, and there are a lot of hours between waking up and falling asleep. Gerald cleaned and straightened until there was nothing left to clean and straighten, then he tried to get his job back, but the contracting business had moved on, far on, from the last time he worked. New graduates, kids, were running the jobs, and besides, it wasn't safe for a seventy-four-year-old to be on a construction site. His hair was white by now, even though he parted it the same way he had when he was thirty. His skin was weathered and wrinkled. Everything around him was new. He didn't fit.

He took an office downtown, a small dusty room with a big window that was full of sun and blue sky in the mornings. He told people he was going to be a freelance writer. He didn't write much–a humor piece for the local tabloid, a few halfhearted attempts at a memoir–mostly he looked out the window and breathed in the musty air. He just liked the rhythm it gave to his life, this waking up and getting ready and going to work and coming home, although every morning it got harder to get off that bench and onto the train. And then he found his pickpocket.

She followed patterns that no one but Gerald knew. She entered from the south entrance, the one with the stairs, rather than the escalator. She skipped down the stairs and moved close to the tracks, leaned her back against a cement pillar. She faced straight down into the black hole of the tunnel, but her eyes darted around, light, searching. She stood at the pillar a few minutes. When the first train came rumbling up the tunnel and the crowds pressed right up to the edge of the track, she drifted in, melted right into the throng, and when the doors hissed open, she made her move. Gerald had seen her unzip purses and unhook wallets from chains while the crowd jostled and shoved. She snatched a silver fountain pen from a stock broker's breast pocket. Plucked a small jewel out of an Indian woman's scarf. Then, as the crowd disappeared behind the sliding doors and was shuttled away from her, she slipped her prizes into some pocket deep in her jacket and slid out the north entrance and was gone until tomorrow.

She was interesting, a diversion, for a while, until the day she pickpocketed the cop. The cop was young and nervous looking, and he stalked around the station every other day and ran out the bums that begged for change. He stood over a bum on a Wednesday morning.

"Got to move along, buddy," he said.

The bum looked up at him. "Come on, man," he said.

"No panhandling in here."

"Cut me a break."

"Don't make this hard," the cop said. He wore a heavy utility belt loaded down with radio and gun and baton and other cop stuff. Everything was held down by leather straps with snaps on them. He unsnapped the pepper spray. "Just move along."

The train rumbled in and the doors opened and the crowd sardined its way into the waiting cars, and as Gerald watched, his pickpocket wove her way in between the people and up behind the cop and snicked the pepper spray right out of his belt and scuttled on out the north entrance. The cop reached for his belt, fumbled thin air, looked down with confusion.

"She got you good, buckaroo," the bum said, grinning a dirty-toothed grin.

Gerald fell in love with her that morning.

Gerald stood at the edge of the crowd with his hand against a pillar. He ran his finger over the cold, gravely cement. The subway station always smelled of metal and soap, of machines and people just out of the shower. A thin man in a suit stood beside Gerald, one of those phone earpiece things attached to him, making him look like a robot. He yelled at whoever was on the other end of the phone, like he was yelling into thin air. Two kids with lunch boxes sat side by side on a bench. One punched the other in the arm and they both laughed.

All around Gerald, the crowd hummed, feet clicking and sticking on the cold ground.

She came in through the south entrance, her sunglasses on, her jackets zipped up against the November cold. She leaned against her pillar. Gerald watched her out of the corner of his eye. He could feel her looking around, looking at him. He slid his hand further up the pillar, his jacket falling further open, his wallet inching out of the inside breast pocket. An inch and a half of leather showing now. She had to see it.

The train snaked into the station. The doors opened. The crowd surged and shoved around him and he looked at her pillar and she was gone. A woman with a bagel smushed into him, got cream cheese on his coat.

"Sorry," she mumbled without looking at him.

The crowd pressed him into the car and the doors shut behind him. Warmth was everywhere, coming from the car's heater, coming from the bodies pressed against each other. Coffee on the air. Gerald felt his pocket. The wallet was gone.

41

The train began to move and the station slid away outside the window. Gerald watched his pickpocket as she edged through the crowd towards the north entrance.

He held onto the metal rail above his head and smiled as the train plowed into the darkness. Graffiti raced by on the tunnel walls. He closed his eyes and pictured his girl, climbing up the stairs and into the cold hard air of the city, scooting along the sidewalk, head down, hands in her pockets while the wind whips her hair around. She turns down an alley and tucks herself into a corner behind a dumpster. She unzips her coat and pulls the wallet out and opens it, rifles through it, stares. No money, no credit cards, no ID. Just a piece of paper. She holds it in her little pink fingers. One side says *BUSTED*. She flips it over. *So audacious. Find me tomorrow.* She huffs, pouts, crumples the paper, sticks it back in her pocket. She fumes. A tiny ball of fire.

Gerald smiled and felt his feet rocking with the train.

She was there the next morning. She leaned against her pillar, her arms crossed, her top teeth biting into her bottom lip. She stared at Gerald. He sat on the bench and stared back while people cut back and forth between them. The subway came and went. She let the crowd and all their wallets and purses and jewelry walk right by in front of her. Then the station was mostly empty, the cashiers were changing shifts, the cop was heading out the north entrance, and the pickpocket padded across the concrete, the soft pat of her shoes echoing around the big room. She stopped in front of him and crossed her arms again.

"What was that all about?" she said.

Gerald smiled at her. He put his palms on the bench and leaned back, crossed one leg over the other. "Surprised?" he said.

"Are you going to turn me in?"

"I wasn't planning on it."

"Then what do you want?"

He looked at her feet. She wore black ballet slippers. "I see you every morning," he said. "Just wanted some company, I suppose."

"Are you trying to hit on me?"

"No."

"How old are you?"

"I'm not trying to hit on you."

"Okay." She looked around the room. A janitor was wandering around with one of those grabber claw things, picking up coffee cups and fruit-bar wrappers. She sat down beside Gerald and pulled the crumpled piece of paper out of her pocket. She looked at it, flipped it over, turned it between her fingers. "What does audacious mean?"

"You've never heard it before?"

"No."

He took the paper from her. "It means daring. Bold."

"So audacious."

"Yup." He handed the paper back to her. She folded it up and slipped it neatly into a pocket. She looked at her feet. Pushed her hair back behind her ears. "I'm Gerald," Gerald said. She nodded. "What's your name?"

She licked her lips. "You think I'm audacious?"

"I do."

"So just call me Audacious."

"You don't have a name?"

"Not that I'm going to tell you."

"Well, Audacious is a little long for a name."

"So shorten it then, whatever. I'm not telling you my real name." She stood up.

"Shorten it? Like, Audi?"

She stood in front of him, zipped her jackets up, first the denim one, then the windbreaker. "Like the car?"

"As in, short for Audacious."

"Fine then. Audi." She turned around, headed for the north entrance.

"See you tomorrow?" Gerald said. His voice bounced off the walls of the station.

She tucked her hands into her jacket and walked out of sight.

He brought her coffee the next morning. Audi stood across the station and stared at him until the train left, then came and sat down beside him. Didn't say a word.

"I thought you'd like it sweet. I put lots of sugar in it. Lots of cream," Gerald said.

She took it from him. "Thanks," she said. She took a sip, licked her lips. "You know, this is two days in a row I've missed a score because of you."

"Whoops."

"You're going to have to help me out if you keep this up," she said. She smiled at him. The gums above her top teeth showed pink and tender. Her dark eyes sparkled. Gerald felt himself filling up inside.

"I brought you coffee," he said. "What else do you want?"

"I'll think of something."

For two weeks she was there every morning. Gerald missed his train to talk to her. He showed up late to the office every day. Not that there was anyone who would notice.

Audi told him about herself. She was twenty-two years old, had been fending for herself for the last six years. She ended up on the street when her boyfriend left her. He owned a house, begged her to move in. She did, and a month later, he'd had enough of her.

"Get your shit and move out, that's all he said to me," Audi said, turning her coffee cup around in her palms. "I knew my parents wouldn't let me back in, they were all pissed off that I left in the first place. So I went downtown to stay with one of my girlfriends. She said there wasn't room, and that was that. I started sleeping in here." She waved her arm, gestured to the cavernous room.

"In the station?" Gerald said.

"Over behind those vending machines. It's warm back there, the machines make it warm, and there's space. And the cops don't look back there."

"Not the most comfortable place in the world though."

"No." She drank her coffee and looked at the vending machines. "But I hung around here enough that I figured people out. And started stealing their stuff. It's easy. And I got enough to pay a sixth of the rent at this place." She told him about the apartment, a place downtown where she stayed with a half-dozen other people her age, the population of the apartment constantly in flux as people disappeared and new ones showed up. She slept on the kitchen floor. Rent was cheap.

44

"And you're happy there?" Gerald said.

"No."

She leaned forward, her paper cup dangling from her fingertips . She scrunched her face and looked at the ground. Her jackets bunched up around her shoulders, her back. Gerald held his hand behind her, an inch from her back, thought about it, watched her, and finally rested his palm flat and gentle against her jacket.

"You know, I've got extra space, if you ever need somewhere to stay," he said.

"I'm not going to have sex with you."

"I'm not asking you to."

"You're old enough to be my granddad."

"Probably so."

He left his hand on her back while another train came and went. Audi was gone the next day. He sat on the bench with a cup of coffee in each hand and watched four crowds get into four trains. Then he went home.

The city turned dark, gray and frigid, as the month wore on. The streets were slick and the tall buildings looked like they were cut from wet cardboard and stuck against the sky.

Each morning Gerald sat at the station, scanning the platform for her, searching the business-coat-wearing, briefcase-toting crowd. He noticed women with their purses hanging loose and open from their shoulders. Men shouting into cell phones while their briefcases sat unwatched beside them. A treasure trove of targets. And no Audi.

Gerald watched through the window of his office as the winter came in fast and cold. The snow blew in sideways and piled in dirty drifts along the edges of the rooftops. The pigeons at first huddled together in the rafters, and eventually disappeared altogether. Gerald tried to fill the hours in the day. He balanced his checkbook. He did crossword puzzles. He wrote, toying around with different stories, far-fetched tales with beautiful female pickpockets as the lead. Mostly he just looked out the window. He wondered if Audi's apartment had a heater. He wondered if she'd really had an apartment to begin with.

45

He went by the market near his house every day on his way home.  He liked putting his hands on the fresh vegetables, weighing the ripe fruit.  He walked slowly, taking his time, planning his meals as he wandered the aisles.  This took time.  Bringing it all home and cooking something also ate up the evening.  By the time everything was eaten and cleaned up, it was almost time to go to bed, and another day was through.

A week before Christmas.  He was sautéing onions when he heard the knock.  He left the onions sizzling in the skillet and went to the door.  Audi was there, the wind blowing cold and wintry around her, her hands deep in her pockets, her ballet shoes wet with dirty snow.

She looked at the ground, made patterns in the sludge with her toe.  "Hi," she said.

"Hi," Gerald said.  He stepped aside and she came in.

He put on a pot of coffee, then he made a huge omelet with eight eggs, green peppers, onions, chopped-up smoked sausage.  Audi sat at the kitchen table with her hands folded in front of her and didn't speak.  She watched him cook.  He cut the omelet in half with the spatula and put half on a plate and set it in front of her.  He sat down with the rest of it and began to eat it right out of the skillet.  Audi stared at her plate.

"You don't like eggs?" Gerald said.

"They're fine," she said.  "It just looks pretty.  I don't want to mess it up."

"It's just an omelet."

"It's been a long time since I've had an omelet."

She ate, and she told him the story, how she'd come home to her apartment and found the door boarded up, how she didn't even know who the landlord was, how she had no idea what happened.  She found one of her roommates on a bench at the park.  He told her the rest.

"Drugs or something," Audi said.  "The guy said that the cops came and busted them, and after that, the landlord kicked everybody out.  Boarded the place up.  Said she'd had enough of renting to worthless kids."

"Shame," Gerald said.  "Not really your fault."

"Hmm."

She finished her plate and he took it from her and put it in the sink. He poured her a cup of coffee and sat back down at the table. She held it tight between her hands.

"How did you find my house?" Gerald said.

"Followed you one day, a few weeks ago." She pushed her hair back. Looked from the cup to Gerald and back again. "You said I could come if I needed to."

"I know I did. And you're welcome to. I just wondered how."

"I don't want to impose."

"You're not."

She drank the coffee. "The food was good," she said.

They sat at the table in silence and drank their coffee. Outside, the snow started to come down again, edging against the windowsill like silent white feathers. Frost coated the glass. The heater kicked on with a groan and the warm air blew through the kitchen. Audi squished her shoes against the tile.

"You want some dry clothes?" Gerald said.

She nodded. Gerald left her at the table and went upstairs. He had a walk-in closet in his bedroom; the right side was full of his stuff, on the left, all of Dolores's clothes still hung where she had left them. He hadn't known what to do with them. Her shoes were lined up neatly against the wall, except for a pair of heavy brown boots–the last shoes she'd worn–thrown haphazard in the corner, exactly where she'd left them. He took a selection of shirts and pants and carried them back downstairs.

Audi was sitting on the couch in the living room when he got back. Gerald laid the clothes out on the coffee table in front of her.

"So retro!" she said, fingering the frilled sleeves of a scarlet blouse. "Where'd you get all this stuff?"

"It was my wife's," Gerald said.

Audi nodded and looked at the clothes.

"She died a few years ago," he went on.

"Of what?"

"Stroke."

Audi picked up a pair of brown slacks and stood up. She held the slacks in front of her and looked down, lifted her leg, twisted her toes. "Do you miss her?"

He nodded. "Often."

"I'm going to put these on," she said. She took the scarlet blouse and the brown slacks and went into the bathroom. She was in there a long time. Gerald turned on the TV. A rerun of *The A-Team* was on. Mr. T beat someone up. Gerald turned down the volume.

"What was her name?" Audi said. She was standing in the doorway, looking slim and clean and young in his wife's clothes.

"Who?"

"Your wife."

"Oh. Dolores. Her name was Dolores."

Audi looked at her reflection in the dark window. "Very pretty," she said, flexing her arm, turning around and standing on her tiptoes. Outside, the snow came down quiet and heavy.

She stayed in the guest bedroom that night. He took the sheets down from the top of the closet and made the bed while she stood in the doorway and watched him. She grinned at him.

"You're pretty good at that, for a guy."

"I had to learn," Gerald said. He tucked the sheets under the corners of the bed.

"My exboyfriend was terrible at it. He always made me help him." She sat down on the end of the bed. "It was a huge pain in the ass."

Gerald propped the pillows against the headboard. "There's a TV," he said, "If you want to watch TV, but I don't have HBO or anything, and I don't know where the remote is."

She crawled up to the top of the bed and settled back into the pillows. "I'll be fine," she said. "I think I'm just going to go on to sleep. I'm tired." She smiled at him. Her skin was fair and her cheeks were flushed and pink. Her hair fell over her eyebrows and spread out behind her on the pillow.

Gerald backed out the door. "Okay, then," he said. "Good night, then." He pulled the door to behind him.

The next day he woke at seven and got dressed. He cracked the door into Audi's room and peaked inside. She lay asleep, under the covers, except for her leg, a long, fleshy leg that hung out and down to the floor, bare and pink. Dolores's pants were on the floor beside the bed. Gerald looked at Audi's skin as she shifted in her sleep. He shook his head and shut the door.

At the office, for the first time in weeks, he found himself compelled to write. He took his latest attempt at a memoir out of the drawer and read the first page. The writing was pedestrian, dull. The scene was a boring one, a school play, from ages ago, from third grade. He folded the pages in half and threw them in the garbage and slid a fresh sheet into the typewriter. He began to write, this time, starting the story with Dolores's death. He wrote with fire, the words crackling like lightning across the page. He saw himself rolling over to the empty part of the bed, relishing the empty space, nuzzling into the pillow as the sun coaxed its way through the windows. Then rising late, stumbling downstairs, where Dolores's hair was splayed across the table, her hands dangling limp and straight down at her sides, milk dripping slowly onto the tile.

And then Audi, a ball of flame in the empty house. He put the paper away and headed home.

She was there when he got back. She was on the couch in another outfit of his wife's, an old sweat suit. She had cooked popcorn and was cuddled up under the blankets, watching TV.

"Enjoying yourself?" Gerald said.

"You know it."

He sat down beside her. She scooted closer. She took a pillow from the end of the couch and set it in his lap, lay her head on top of it, and turned on her side to keep her eyes on the TV. She was watching a music video.

"What did you do today?" Gerald asked her.

"This," she said. "All day. Bummed around. It was great." She laughed. It was the first time he'd heard her laugh, a tinkling wind-chime sort of sound that started in her chest and bounced its way across her tongue. It put tingles in Gerald's spine. "How about you?" she said.

"I did some writing."

"What about?"

"About you."

She turned over on her back and looked up at him. "You're writing about me?"

49

"Yup." He watched the TV. The band was playing in a warehouse. He could feel her eyes on him, cold and intense.

"You better write me exciting. I don't want to be a boring character."

"You're not."

"And I better be pretty," she said. Then she turned back to the TV.


She stayed with him. He went to his office and wrote, and came home and talked to her about his day. He spent all day looking forward to his time on the couch with her, to the feeling of the weight of her head on his lap, the feeling of her breath so near his face.

He stayed home on Christmas day. He was cooking biscuits when she came downstairs, slow and sleepy-eyed.

"Merry Christmas," Gerald said.

She sat down at the table and yawned. "Don't say *Merry* Christmas," she said. "It sounds so commercial."

"What do you want me to say?"

"How about *Happy* Christmas, like you say for every other holiday?"

"Fine, *Happy* Christmas. Honey or jelly? On your biscuits."

"Honey."

"Good choice." He put the biscuits in the oven and took the honey from the cabinet and set it on the table in front of her. "They'll take a few minutes to cook."

"I got you a Christmas present," she said. She looked at the table and wrung her hands. "I'm not sure if you'll like it."

"What is it?"

"You promise you'll like it? Or at least say you'll like it?"

"I promise I'll at least say I like it."

"You smart ass," she said. She ran upstairs and came back down with a brown paper bag and handed it to Gerald. She sat back at the table and waited.

Gerald opened the bag. There was a picture frame inside. He pulled it out. Inside the frame was the piece of paper that he'd left for her in his wallet, the side with the *audacious* bit on it. She'd taken colored pencils and traced over all the creases from where she'd crumpled the paper up, then she colored the sections all different colors. It looked like the dry, cracked ground in the desert would look if someone attacked it with a paintbrush. The word *audacious* was traced in brilliant red. The colors were amplified behind the glass of the frame. Gerald turned it between his fingers.

"You like it?" Audi said.

"I love it," Gerald said. He propped it up on the table in front of him.

"You promise?"

"I love it." He looked at her. She was blushing, her face turned away from him. "I didn't get you anything," he said. "I can get you something."

"You don't have to," she said. "You've done plenty."

They spent the entire day on the couch, watching the Christmas shows–Rudolph, Frosty, Island of Lost Toys–until it got dark outside and the snow started to fall. Gerald went upstairs and got into bed. He closed his eyes.

He didn't know how long he had been asleep when Audi came in. He felt her as soon as she came into the room. Gerald watched her. She was wearing a t-shirt and panties. She tiptoed across the carpet to the side of the bed, then she pulled the covers back a bit and slid under them. She cuddled up close beside him, put one of her bare legs across his. Her legs felt smooth and soft. She pulled Gerald's arm up above his head and put her head on his chest, wrapped her arm across his stomach. Gerald felt her hair on his chin. He felt her eyelashes on his chest. His muscles tensed.

"You've been really sweet to me, Gerald," she said.

He let his arm drop slowly. He brought it around her and pulled her close to him. She wrapped her leg around him and squeezed back.

"I could fall in love with you," she said.

"No, you can't," he whispered. He breathed in her hair; she smelled of honey and apples and skin. Then he kissed her on the top of her head. She looked up at him, her eyes dark points in the dark room. She inched forward and kissed him on the mouth, twice, feather soft. Then she lay her head back on his chest and fell asleep. Gerald stared at the ceiling and listened to her breathing.

He woke up and the sun was bright on her face. He shook her. She stirred and batted her eyes and looked at him.

"Hey," she said.

"Get up," he said. "I want to take you somewhere. Late Christmas present."

She rolled off of him onto her back, bunched the covers up over her face. "I'm still sleepy," she said, her eyes peeking out above the bedspread.

"You want me to make you some breakfast?"

"Make me some more biscuits," she said. "Just do it quietly." She grinned at him, then she flopped over in the bed and covered her head with the pillow.

Gerald walked downstairs and looked in the refrigerator. He was out of milk. He put on his boots and his coat and his hat and walked outside. The air was crisp and stung his nostrils. The sun glinted off the icicles that hung from the eaves of his house.

He put his hands in his pockets and walked up the street to the market. The electric doors slid open and bathed him in warmth and fluorescence. He smiled at the cashier and walked to the back and took a carton of milk from the shelf. He turned it over in his hand, checked the expiration date. He looked at the back of the carton, where they put the announcements about missing children. Audi's picture was printed in smudged ink beneath the nutrition information.

Gerald stared at it. Her eyes looked back at him from the cold cardboard. Nikki Tyler, age sixteen, runaway, missing since she was fourteen. Height. Weight. Parents' number and address. Her parents live just forty-five minutes outside the city, less than an hour from Gerald's house.

He put the carton on the shelf and chose a different one, one with a picture of a little black boy on the back, and bought it and took it home.

Audi was on the couch watching *The Price is Right*. "Took you long enough," she said. She had the blankets tented around her, just her head sticking out, her eyes intent on the TV. Her nose was small in profile, her lips thin and pink. She turned to him, smiled. "You miss me?"

Gerald shifted the milk from one hand to the other. "Terribly," he said.

52

He cooked the biscuits and they ate some in front of the TV, then they packed a lunch and got in the car and headed north on the interstate. The roads were empty. The new snow was flat all around them, mostly smooth, but whipped by the wind in some places until it looked like peaked meringue. The sky was deep blue and far away. Audi pressed her nose against the window as they drove.

"Where are we going?" she said.

"*Ultima Thule*," Gerald said.

"What?"

"End of the Earth."

They pulled into a parking lot beside a huge frozen lake. Gerald got out of the car and opened the trunk and took out a blanket and their food. They set off toward the lake. Gerald stepped gently off the sand and onto the ice; it held firm.

"Careful," he said. He took Audi's hand in his. They walked across the ice, their footprints sitting deep in the powdery snow.

"It's like walking on the moon," she said, her hand tight in his, warm, her eyes scanning the blue horizon. Her feet were soft on the ice.

A hundred yards off shore, Gerald spread out the blanket and sat down. He handed Audi a sandwich. They ate and looked out over the lake. The ice was cracked and shattered not far from where they sat, and beyond that, there were huge gaps with water in between them. Silvery blue and white floes were broken off and drifting beyond, spaced further and further out toward the blue horizon.

"I used to take my wife here," Gerald said. "She liked it. She said it was like the world was trying to stay together, but it was too much. The pull of whatever's outside the world was too much, and it made the earth just break apart and float away."

"That's very pretty," Audi said.

"She said when we were here, she felt like we were sitting on the very edge."

Audi nodded and chewed her sandwich. She took Gerald's hand in hers and held it in her lap and squeezed it tight. The air was still and cold. Water birds cackled at the edge of the lake. The ice cracked and groaned.

"Audi," Gerald said, "what are you going to do?" He watched the birds as they pecked around in the snow. He felt Audi looking at him.

"What do you mean?" she said.

"I mean, with yourself?" He felt her put her other hand on his, closing his rough hand in her fists. "Don't you miss your parents?"

"They were mean to me, Gerald."

"Were they really? Is that why you left?"

She squeezed his hands. "I'm not going to lie to you," she said. They watched the ice float out over the deep water.

They headed home as the sun started to go down. The sky was cloudless and clean; the sun turned the horizon a bright yellow orange as the light reflected off the snow and the ice. Audi leaned back in the passenger seat and shut her eyes.

"I'm stopping up here at this rest area," Gerald said.

Audi mumbled something, her voice heavy with sleep.

"You got to pee?"

She shook her head. Gerald pulled off the interstate and into a parking place at the rest area. He left the car on and the heater running. He used the restroom and came outside and stood in the cold, watching his breath form clouds in front of his face. In the parking lot, a family rearranged the contents of their van.

Gerald shook his right leg, then his left. They felt stiff from the drive. He took some long steps around the rest area. He wandered over to the drink machines and bought a Coke. He opened it and took a sip and walked back to the kiosk with the map and the advertisements. He looked over the adds for car insurance and get-rich-quick jobs. In the top right corner were six pieces of paper with pictures of people on them, flyers advertising missing children, the rest-area equivalent of the back of a milk carton. Audi's was in the middle. He read her parents' address again, looked back at the car in the parking lot. The headlights were on and steam was easing out from under the hood. In the woods behind, the snow lay heavy on the limbs of the trees. The branches crackled with ice.

Audi slept in the passenger seat. Her mouth was open slightly and her right temple leaned against the window. She had her legs tucked into her chest and her arms pulled inside the sleeves of her shirt. Gerald turned the heater up and looked out the window. The dark in front of him grew brighter as the inky night slid past, and then the city rose up glowing and hard in front of them. He left the interstate and headed into the neighborhood.

Gerald drove slowly, scanning the dark houses for the address. The houses were small and weathered; the streets were lined with ghostly bare trees. The wind picked up outside and tossed snowflakes off the ground and into the air. It ripped and whistled around the car. Audi woke up. She yawned and scratched her nose, looking around. She stared out the window.

"What are we doing here?" she said.

Gerald didn't say anything. He turned the brights on to see through the swirling snow.

"Gerald. Where are we going?" Audi was glaring at him. Her eyes piercing neat holes in the side of his head.

"I'm taking you home," Gerald said.

"I don't live around here."

"I'm taking you back to your parents, Nikki."

Audi sat up straight in the chair. "You son of a bitch," she said. "You knew? How long have you known?"

"Only a little while—"

"Have you been planning this? Is this your trick? Your trick to get me back to my parents?" She climbed onto her knees in the seat, one hand on the dashboard, the other on the headrest, and put her face close to Gerald's, yelling at him. "They rewarding you or something? Are you some sort of bounty hunter?"

"I only found out today," Gerald said. He stopped at a stop sign and looked at her. "I just found out."

"I don't want to go back. I told you they were mean to me."

Gerald sighed. "I know, Audi. But you've told me a lot of stuff."

"You son of a bitch."

"I just want to do what's best for you," he said. He started to pull forward.

"Stop the car," Audi said.

"What—"

55

"Stop the car!" She yelled it right in his ear. Gerald stopped and Audi sat back down in the seat. She looked out the windshield. The wind rocked the car and the snow made wispy patterns in the dark air. "Who the hell are you to say what's best for me," she said.

Gerald sat quietly for a moment. The engine vibrated; snow melted on the hood. The air from the heater felt fusty and warm on his face. "I don't know. I don't know."

She didn't look at him. She stared down at her shoes. After a while, she said, "You don't want to keep me?"

She was so small in the chair. She had her knees pulled into her shirt again.

"You know I can't, Nikki," Gerald said.

She turned to him. Her eyes were wet pieces of coal. "Stop calling me that," she said. She opened the door and the cold swirled through the car. She got out and zipped her jacket tight around her and slammed the door behind her. She walked up the street.

Gerald reached across the center console and struggled to roll the window down. "Nikki," he yelled after her. "Nikki, hang on. Audi! Audi." He checked the intersection and put the car in gear and swung around the corner after her, but when he looked up again, she was gone, disappeared into the dark, into wind and the cold.

Gerald got home and the house was empty and quiet. Upstairs, Dolores's clothes, the ones that Audi had worn, were scattered across the floor. The bed was unmade. He left it all there. In the kitchen, the remains of the biscuits sat in the sink. His Christmas present, Audi's artwork, *audacious*, lay on the kitchen table. He picked it up and carried it into the living room and propped it on the TV.

Outside, the wind had died down and the snow was falling again. He wrapped up in a blanket and sat down on the couch and closed his eyes. The heater clicked on. Gerald listened to its ticks and pings and rumbles as the heat snuck through the empty rooms.

My son was already there when I got home from work. He didn't look at me when I came in. He was sitting at the computer, chewing on a piece of pizza. The pizza box lay open on the floor beside him. I hung my hat on the rack and sat down at the kitchen table and started unlacing my boots.

"Your mother left already?" I said.

"Yeah. She just dropped me." He had his elbow resting on the arm of the chair, the pizza crust dangling idly from his fingers. He clicked away with the mouse.

"She have anything to say?"

"No."

I threw my boots into the corner and pulled off my socks. It was November, one of the first cold days of the year, and raining outside. My toes were pruned. The tile felt cold under my feet. "Pass me some of that pizza?" I said. My son slid the box across the floor. I picked up a slice and leaned back in the chair. "I'd have cooked you something, you know."

"I was hungry," my son said.

"You could have waited."

"You were like an hour late."

We ate our pizza. I brushed the crumbs off of my lap and onto the floor. I grabbed another slice and stood behind him, leaned on the back of the chair. He'd thrown my mail on the floor to make room for his plate. Bills scattered across the carpet. "You made a mess," I said.

"Well there's no room for anything else with your shit all over the place."

"Don't cuss."

"Whatever." He flipped the crust across the room and it landed on the floor next to the box.

I looked at the computer screen. On it was a picture of the Earth, all blue and green, with black behind it. "What you looking at?" I said.

"Google Earth." He wiped some dust off the screen.

"What's it do?"

"It's cool. Check it out." He clicked the mouse and spun the earth around, spinning it like a globe, until we were looking at the whole of the western hemisphere. Then he rolled the wheel on the mouse and the view on the screen ticked in, in until America took up the whole screen, and he kept zooming in until I could see the white of the sands along the coast of Florida.

"It's satellite pictures," my son said.

"That's right now? What we're seeing is what it looks like right now?" I said.

"No, it's old pictures. Taken over months. Then they put them back together into this. Here's the house." He had zoomed all the way in onto our city and into the neighborhood where I lived, all the way down to the L-shaped roof of my house. I could see my pickup in the driveway, the motorboat full of leaves on the trailer in the back yard. "Cool, huh?" he said.

I stared at the screen. "We're in there?"

"Maybe. Depends on when the picture was taken. We might have been somewhere else."

Something about that bothered me. I didn't know what. He zoomed out and panned the view around the town; we saw the boatyard where I worked. My son's high school. The softball fields where we used to play on weekends. The satellites caught them all. Fields and buildings and roads and cars and not a person anywhere. Everything was deserted.

"How did you find out about this?" I said.

"Mom showed me. I think she's been teaching with it in class, having her students use it."

"Your mom was always better with that kind of thing than I was. The technology stuff."

"Wouldn't hurt you to figure it out," he said. "Okay, so if you could go anywhere in the world, where would you go?"

"You mean other countries?"

"Anywhere. Where do you wish you could go?" He looked at me for a second and then he said, "Never mind. Look. Just check it out."

My son took the camera to China, and he zoomed in on Hong Kong. I could see the tent roofs of a marketplace. Junks and barges were tied together, brown and blue and floating side-by-side, hundreds of them in the bay. Then he went to Australia and scanned around the outback, miles of desert scrolling yellow on the screen, until he stopped on a giant brown rock, squatting like a toad in the middle of the sand.

"That's Ayers Rock," he said. "So you see what I'm talking about?" he said. "You can see anywhere." He took the cameras to the Amazon, where the river flowed through green jungles. The jungle seemed endless–tangled and deep–and I thought that there must be huge areas in there where no one had ever walked.

"I guess I always wanted to go to Europe," I said. "I was going to live in Italy, in Rome."

He spun the Earth around and centered on the boot-shaped country. "Why didn't you?"

"They were taking some guys over there for a job, back when I was working for the construction company. But I never got around to filling out the paperwork, getting the passport, you know."

"That sucks."

"Well, things worked out okay." I picked the pizza crust off the floor and put it in the garbage. Then I stood behind him again.

"Still," he said. He zoomed in on Rome. The camera caught a bunch of people crowding the plaza in front of a big church; the satellite view made them look like fleas caught in a hairless patch on a dog.

"Must have been a Wednesday," my son said.

"Why?"

"That's the *Piatza di San Pietro*, out in front of St. Peter's. Where the Pope lives. He talks on Wednesdays. They're out there listening to him." He zoomed in further. "Can't see him. He's probably standing right there on that balcony."

I looked at the crowd and thought of a satellite, alien and spiny, coasting silently a hundred miles above their heads, the camera's shutter clicking quiet over the lens. I wondered if the satellites got in the way of the people's prayers, messed them up on their way to heaven. Maybe God was only hearing static.

"You can see everything and everyone," my son said.

"Where am I?"

"Somewhere." He leaned back in the chair, his hand on the mouse, aimlessly dragging the view over southern Europe.

"Where?"

"You're there, okay?" He folded his hands behind his neck and stared at me, shaking his head. "You're there, somewhere."

I squinted at the screen. Then I dragged a chair across the chipped tile floor and sat down beside him. "Go back to the boatyard," I said. He focused on the boatyard again–the freighter ships, the trucks, the train tracks and the forklifts–everything empty and still. The parking lot, the office where I punched my time card, and the yard itself; all of it fit into the screen. Tractor-trailer-sized boxes of cargo dotted the view like Lego blocks. No people, anywhere.

It wasn't until a few days later, when my son had gone back to his mother's and I was waiting at a red light on my way home from work, that I realized what had bothered me that afternoon.

Assume I'm in one of those pictures, somewhere, just indoors so the satellite didn't see me. Then that's one thing. But what if the satellite took the picture of my house while I was at work, and the picture of my work while I was at home? Then there's *not* a picture of me; as far as Google Earth is concerned, I'm not part of the world. I'm stuck in the seams between the photographs, off the map somewhere. The satellites are blinking by overhead, ignoring me. Everything's spinning on without me.

# GHOSTS ON THE RIVER

The bay's a ragged blue and white with the wind ripping foam off the tops of the waves. We're at the yacht club, like we are every day in the summer, and we're sprinting barefoot on the concrete dock. We're running shoreward, past the sailboats floating in their slips, halyards pinging against the masts, past the long green yard where we play football, past the deck where our parents drink margaritas and watch us, we're sprinting barefoot all the way to the window of the dining room because Horace is in there.

Horace is big and lumpy and worn; he looks much older than my mom, even though he was in the same classes as her up until fourth grade. He has short brown hair with a long, curved white line going from his left eye over his ear and around the back of his head. The hair doesn't grow there. He's at the corner table where he eats lunch every afternoon, and his mother–old and white haired and hunched–cuts his food for him, brings the fork to his mouth airplane-to-hanger style. She tucks a napkin into the collar of his shirt.

The glass is tinted and we cup our hands around our faces to see through. Horace's mother doesn't look at us. Horace does. Horace turns his head and the mashed potatoes bump into his cheek. He looks at us, his eyes dark and vacant. Then he closes his eyes and shuts his mouth so tight that little lines stick out the sides of his lips. His mother starts rubbing his head, trying to calm him down, but it's not working. Horace opens his mouth in a big dark O and starts wailing this loud, primal-type hollering that everyone else in the dining room pretends not to hear. He does this and we jump and run away and laugh and call him a wounded walrus. Then we run right back out onto the water and off the end of the dock, yelling the whole way, concrete hot on our feet and then water cool and clean all around us.

My parents tell me it's rude to make fun of Horace because he can't help the way he is. He was a normal little boy, just like me, they say, until his accident. He was run over by a boat, chopped in the head with the prop. He almost died. His brain hadn't worked right since. He'd never live a normal life or get married or have a family; even if by some miracle he met a woman, he could never have kids–other important parts of him had been chewed up in that hunk of whirling metal.

So Horace is supposed to be an example to us. Our parents tell us we should be careful, as if by saying these words we will do something different than whatever it was we were going to do anyway.


The father-son camping trip was becoming a tradition, with me and Jimmy and Tem and Robbie and Ben, and all of our dads. The first year, when I was eleven, we went to Lake Marshall, a blue spring-fed hole in the white sands of the Florida Panhandle. I stepped on a piece of glass and gouged a hook-shaped hole in the bottom of my foot. Jimmy's dad was a doctor. He stitched me up by the campfire.

When I was twelve we camped out by the Econfina river. We jumped from bluffs near one of the deepest springs. I slipped on the wet moss at the top and tumbled end over end into the water. Bruises the size of oranges.

This year was the most extravagant: a fishing trip on the Apalachicola River. My friends said, "How you going to kill yourself this time?"

In my head, the river was just a piece of sightseeing, hanging like a brown ribbon far below as we crossed the bridge over it, on the way to Tallahassee or some other place east of home. Close up, it was different, warm and slow moving and colored like sweet tea. Water bugs skitted along the surface in the calm parts near the shore. We stood on the riverbank and looked into the brown water while our dads launched the boats.

We headed down the river, our mini-armada. A father and a son to each boat, my dad and I in an aluminum johnboat we had rented. I sat near the bow and looked over into the water while my dad steered. The water curled in crazy patterns off the flat front of the hull. There were bugs and weeds and pieces of sticks floating along in the river; the bow wake swallowed them up and spit them out in a frothy mess.

The trees were far away on either side of the wide river. A barge passed us on its way upstream. A man in the cabin of the tugboat waved to us.

The fishing lodge sat on a dark bend in the river, an old building of sagging wet wood. We tied the boats up to the dock and carried our junk inside. We claimed bunk beds on the screen porch while the water whispered below us. Then we did cannonballs into the river while our dads drank beer on the dock.

The sun went down and Tem's dad cooked fried chicken. It sizzled in the oil in the deep pan and the salty summer smell drifted all over the cabin. We sat outside and ate and watched the night come in. In the cloud-struck twilight, the moon was a flashlight behind blue gauze, and the darkness raced across the river like the childhood nightmares of the sun. Robbie's dad leaned back in his chair. He was older than the rest of our dads, tall and lean with curly gray hair. He smiled and rested his hands on his belly.

"Haints'll be out tonight," he said.

We kids looked at each other. Robbie looked embarrassed. Jimmy was giggling. "Haints?" he said.

"Haints," Mr. Blue went on. "Spooks. Ghosts."

"It's like slang for haunts," Ben's dad said.

"They come out when the moon's like this," Robbie's dad said. "Especially near the river. Any time you're near the water. Because the water's just one big graveyard."

We were quiet. The tree frogs whirred, winding up to a noise that went through the ears and into the middle of the skull. Robbie's dad waited for them to quiet down. He looked out over the deep river.

"You know where that river goes?" he said.

"The Gulf," I said.

"That's right. The Apalach flows all the way out into the Gulf. And the Gulf flows into the Atlantic, and all over the world. It's all one thing, one big water no matter how you break it down. And the haints know that. All of them. All the ones that died at sea, all over the world, they can all slip around under the surface and go wherever they want. And they love it when the moon's out like this."

The frogs started crying again and we watched the shadows move on the water. We went to bed late and listened to the nighttime noises outside, the whispers and the moans of the dark

63

forest, and we tried to go to sleep with the river moving beneath us.

In the morning we woke up with the heavy smell of bacon in the air. I went into the kitchen and Tem's dad was frying eggs that popped and slid around in the grease the bacon left in the pan. "Where yall going today?" he said.

"I think we're going downriver," I said.

We all ate together at a long table and talked about our fishing plans. Then my dad and I untied the boat and headed downriver to where we thought the fish might be. We motored up into feeder creeks and eddies where the water was still and clear, not the brown, heavy-flowing stuff of the big river. We went up into quiet inlets where the grass stuck up out of the water like green knives and the cypress knees clanked against the aluminum hull. If I was a fish, that is where I would be. We had worms in a white Tupperware and crickets in a cage that they couldn't find their way out of, even though there was a giant hole right in the top for you to reach in and grab them.

I dropped the line into the water and watched the bait sit a few inches below the clear surface. Bream and crappie swam up and looked at the bait and swam away.

"They're not eating it," I said.

My dad sat near the stern and looked at his own line. He didn't say anything.

"What are we supposed to do? We doing it wrong?"

"I don't know," he said. "I don't know why they're not biting."

"This is boring." I said.

"I can't control the fish."

We sat in silence. Something big and fast bounded around in the woods, out of sight. A squirrel sat in a tree and watched us. It held a pinecone in its tiny claws. It plucked a scale off the pinecone and ate the seed, then dropped the scale to the ground. It landed in the pine straw with a faint pat. I pulled my line out of the water and sat with my arms crossed over my knees.

"Can I try driving the boat?"

"What for?" my dad said. He was pulling his line in too.

"I don't know. Something to do. Jimmy's dad was letting him drive."

My dad motored back out into the middle of the river and we switched places. "Take it nice and easy," he said to me. The motor didn't have a steering wheel, just a tiller with a twist-on throttle. It was hard to control the speed; a twist too hard made the boat jerk forward, too soft made the boat slow and bog down. The tiller trembled and jerked in my hand, the water flowing by underneath and trying to snatch it out of my grasp. It was fun.

We went back to the lodge and ate lunch. We convinced our dads to let us take the boats out without them. Jimmy and Ben took Ben's Boston Whaler. Tem and Robbie were in Tem's jonboat. I took our rented boat out alone.

We drove slowly away from the dock until we got out onto the wide river and opened the engines up. We went upstream for a while, passed a barge heading downriver to the Gulf. We cruised around in an offshoot, slaloming the shattered stumps until the eddy dead-ended into a swamp, then Tem and Robbie and I went back out into the big water. Ben and Jimmy were hanging back, looking at something.

We bobbed side by side in the middle of the river, engines rumbling in idle. Tem looked downriver. Nothing but flat brown water ahead of us. "You want to race?" he said.

I looked across the bow. The river curved a mile or so away from us. Smoke from the barge drifted into the air, far in the distance. "Where to?"

"I don't know. 'Til somebody wins."

Robbie was chuckling in the swivel chair on the bow.

"All right," I said. I shifted my butt on the seat and tightened my grip on the throttle.

"On your mark," Tem said, "get set, go!"

We took off. The engine roared and the bow rose into the air for a moment, then splashed down as the boat planed off. Water splashed all around me and into my face. Tem and Robbie were cruising along beside me. My boat was smaller and less powerful than Tem's. My engine was only twenty-five horsepower, and I had no steering wheel, just the tiller. Tem and his forty-horse motor and his nice steering wheel were pulling ahead of me quick, leaving me in their root beer-tinted wake.

Robbie was laughing in the bow. I decided that racing was stupid, and that I should go back and see what Ben and Jimmy were doing.

I pulled the tiller hard to the left, felt the water catch the prop funny, the bow swing violently to the right and the boat change course way too fast. All twenty-five horses went from pushing me forward to pushing in a circle in an instant; it felt like giant heavy hands were tugging on my shoulders, and I went flying right out of the boat.

I was in the air, upside down, then I was in the water, and the water was hot and sulfurous all around me. I bobbed once and watched the boat as it kept on going, the engine stuck in full throttle, the boat swinging around in a tight circle, completing its first solo revolution. The shore was a mass of green far behind it, and the sky so blue and far away. The gunmetal hull glinted in the sun, and then the boat came back, straight at me. The flat front of the bow came at me in a narrow arc and tore by right in front of my face. Water splashed off the hull and into my hair. I felt the turbulence of the prop on my shins, water and bubbles smooth over my skin like the jet of a Jacuzzi. Then the boat was past and on its next circle, and I started trying to backpaddle away from it.

I was downriver of the boat. The water was carrying us along together, drawing us in tandem toward the Gulf. The boat came around again, the engine whining and echoing off the surface. The corner of the bow clipped my shin–I felt the skin tear and the blood come up liquid and warm–and I tucked my knees into my chest as the engine and the wild propeller ripped by again. I went into full backstroke mode, arms flailing behind me and legs kicking while the boat kept spinning. My eyes burned and my ears were full of water but I could still see the boat spinning relentless, hear the engine screaming.

Then I had one of those moments, one when time slows down. It was like the time I fell from forty feet up in the bayleaf tree and counted the branches that I banged against on the way down. Or the time that my mother drove the car into the concrete median of I-275, and I held my breath as the airbags inflated and the car spun around and I waited for the bus or the Mack truck to hit me. I was lucid.

The boat came around for the third time, and with the sun bright and the water cradling me as I swam, I saw someone in the driver's seat. He looked like he had been dragged up from the dark bottom of the Gulf. His skin was white as the moon and wrinkled, and his body was lined and creased with pink scars. He was naked, and between his legs where he should have been a man was nothing, nothing but more scar tissue. He looked at me with eyes vacant and deep and cold as outer space, eyes filled with all the water in all the oceans, and I saw that it was Horace; he stared through me and gunned the engine and opened his mouth into a silent scream.

I tucked into a ball again and the bow hit me on the shoulder and rocked me, shoved me out of the way as the boat roared on. Then Tem and Robbie were there, they were there and they pulled me out of the water and drove us out of the way.

I sat in the bow of Tem's boat. My shin was bruised and bleeding. My shoulder ached. Tem looked at me, his eyes wide and scared. Robbie was cracking up.

The boat spun on by itself, drifting, tearing circles in the middle of the river.


We are older now and we still play at the yacht club. We do back flips off the pilings. The water always catches us.

Jimmy stands on the dock. He looks toward shore. "Wounded walrus!" he yells. "Hey guys, wounded walrus!"

Everyone scrambles out of the water, pulls themselves belly-first onto the dock. The concrete is rough on my skin. We run down the dock and across the grass and up to the window of the yacht club dining room. We look in. Horace is just sitting down. He looks at me.

There's something else Robbie's dad told us, while we sat out there under the moon by the river and he told us about the haints and the water and the big graveyard. "That water," he said, "That water goes out into the Gulf and evaporates. It turns into storms and rains all over the state, all over the town, in the reservoir, even. You drink it. It's part of you." He leans back and lets the moon light his face. "Everything that was ever part of the water is a part of you."

Horace looks at me with those dark and empty eyes, and I can feel him cutting through the glass between us, I can feel him in the soft spot on my shoulder, the scar on my knee. I can feel him in my veins.

# PEAK

The morning that he died, Roger spent longer than usual shaving. He took the usual amount of time wetting the bristles of the shaving brush he'd had since he retired, the usual length of time to stir the chalky disk of soap at the bottom of his mug into a froth and spread it across his face. He spent the extra time looking in the mirror, paused between his third and fourth razor strokes on the right side of his face, about half-way between the corner of his mouth and the end of his white sideburn. He was tugging the skin on his face, pulling it taut so that the razor would run smooth, just like Jake, his barber, used to do. It had been 17 years since Jake died, since he collapsed on the floor in the middle of giving a shave–remembering, in the throes of a heart attack, to keep the razor from nicking the client–and so it had been 17 years since Roger had a professional shave. And it occurred to him, looking in the mirror, that 17 years ago he had had his *last* professional shave. The last one of his life. And this was what got him thinking and taking longer than normal to shave his face.

He'd been 70 when he had that last shave, and if he had known that he'd be looking in the mirror when he was 87 and shaving himself not-quite-so-close and wishing Jake could rake the razor over him again, he might have enjoyed it a little more. Maybe the blade would have felt a little sharper, the steaming towel a little hotter.

It had been 19 years since he taught his last class. He was a high school teacher, taught algebra to $10^{th}$ graders for most of his life. Taught the numbers until the numbers came to own him, to define everything he did. Everything was a number in relation to everything else, if you looked at it in the right way. The sun is 23 degrees above the horizon. Roger's right arm is .34 inches longer than his left. His students' hearts beat, on average, 8 times per minute more than his. And looking in the mirror in the fog of 87 years, the math is there for him, the numbers crystalized somewhere in his brain, and he can tick off the years as clearly and quickly as an auctioneer:

19 years since he taught his last class.

4 years since the last time he spent Christmas in his own house. But he never figured that the last time was the last time.

12 years since the last time he went sailing. But that time hadn't even been that good, he remembered. The wind was shifty and the boat drifted slow and hot. The water smelled of dead things. It was not the best sailing trip that he had been on. He couldn't remember the best sailing trip he had been on. But he knew that when he went on it, he had no idea that it was the best, just like when he went on the last one he had no idea it would be his last.

65 years since he ran his fastest mile, 5:14; not amazing, but respectable, at least.

59 years since he had sex with the most beautiful woman he'd ever meet, an actress, blonde and way out of his league, a windfall in the smoky bar. 44 years since the best sex he'd had, with the woman he'd cheated with for years and years. 23 years since he'd made love to his wife. 3 years since his wife had recognized him.

He could see all of these best moments, stretching out like a string of Christmas lights, back and back, back as far as the numbers could take him, each and every best a glowing spark in his life. Looking in the mirror at his gray face, half covered in dripping shaving cream, he thought about how he had missed every single one of those bests. And now he was at the end of the string of lights, and if he told anyone about this he'd get some sickeningly cheerful response, probably from his granddaughter, along the lines of "at the end of every string there's a plug to connect a whole new bunch of lights!" But Roger had never felt so much like the blunt green plug at the end of the string, dangling with nothing between him and the ground but cold December air.

35 years since the high point of his career, winning the local Teacher of the Year award. Local. Only one high school in the county, one school with 28 teachers.

80 years since the smartest he ever felt, when he beat his older brother in a game of chess.

61 years since he felt the most content, sitting alone on a beach by the Gulf, watching a shrimp boat coast silently past, the water as green and still as he'd ever seen it.

He started shaving again, slowly, the razor prickling over the bumps and wrinkles on his skin. Up and down, like hills, like mountains.

Time is like a mountain range, he thought. Peaks and valleys, peaks and valleys over and over forever. Or not forever. And somewhere along there, there's a peak higher than all the rest—the most furious burning bulb, if you like that analogy better. Roger slid the razor in short strokes just below his nose, took out the trace of a mustache. He thought about how at some point he was there, he was standing on that highest peak, the high-point of his life, and he didn't even know it. Because it wasn't the teaching award, or screwing the actress. He'd have known if those were the high-points.

He thought about astronauts and Olympic athletes, and how they had it so easy. For them the peak is so high, an Everest, an Olympus Mons of life: walking on the moon or standing on the top step of the podium and they have nowhere to look but down. But that thought, the knowing that there is nowhere to go but down, made Roger shiver and nick his chin. He'd had his peak, but he didn't know it at the time, and that made all the difference. Because anything could have been the peak, or the peak could still be coming, and that made life worth living. And now at the end of his life, he thought he knew where it was, the peak. And it wasn't his wedding or the birth of his son or his retirement party. And it wasn't when he felt the happiest or the smartest or the most in love, just when he felt the *most*.

It was a day when he was 23 years old, 64 years ago. It was during the war, and he was in a forest on the outer edges of Germany. It was winter, cold, and snow was coming down heavy from the low gray sky. He and a few other men from his platoon were on a patrol, and they walked, spread out side-by-side, through a forest. The trees were black and old, dense. The ground was white and the snow made the air white and he couldn't see but a few feet in front of his face. The forest was silent; the snow crunched softly under their feet.

They walked up a hill, and at the top the trees stretched out in front of them on the downslope, the snow pure and flat between them. Then, not ten feet from Roger, a German soldier stepped out from behind a tree. He held his rifle in the crook of his elbow, and he was zipping up his fly. He looked at Roger and twitched his nose and brought his gun to his shoulder in a slow, smooth motion. They stood facing each other, the barrels of their guns nearly touching. The soldier's breath hung in quick little clouds in front of his face. His eyes were blue and wide. He licked his lips; his finger quivered on the trigger.

Then Roger shot him. The German fell back into the snow hard, like he'd been hit by a battering ram. The bullet had hit him near the clavicle, and blood came up and got red all over the snow. The soldier's breathing was shallow. He was looking at Roger, trying to pull a glove off of his hand. Then he died. The other men in Roger's platoon stood looking at the body.

"If you hadn't of shot him soon, I'd have done it myself," one said. "Hell of a nice shot though. You had him lights out in ten seconds flat."

Roger looked down at the German soldier. His upper teeth were clamped down hard on his lip. His helmet had fallen off and rolled a little way down the hill; frost was already crisping on the tips of his hair. The blood melted the snow and sunk in deep into the earth. The soldier looked about Roger's age, and he looked very dead. He was dead, Roger thought, because I shot first. Roger was alive and breathing, standing with the leather soles of his boots between him and the cold snow, his buddies gawking at the sprawled-out soldier and laughing and giving congratulatory pats on the back. Roger was alive and he felt alive–alive by a half-second, his finger a tiny bit faster while the German was dead.

A few hours before he died, Roger remembered this while he looked in the mirror, and 64 extra years of life coursed through his veins while the ghost of what might have been resonated in his bones.

# BLOODHOUND

It's never until the third day, late in the second day at the earliest, that they call for us. The first day is spent calling friends, neighbors, everyone a person can think of in hopes that the Missing is not really missing, just off dallying somewhere they're not supposed to be. The second day is the local manhunt, when all of the Missing's friends and family scour the area, calling the person's name, some of the local cops joining in after a while.

After they've exhausted that option, when most of the hope is gone and the parents or husbands or whatever are squint-eyed and red-faced in desperation, they call me and Ruckus, and more likely than not, we're going to find the Missing. It's a thrill for Ruckus every time; no matter what he finds, he gets his cookie, his scratch behind the ears, his *Good boy! Good dog!* And whatever we find, someone will tell me good job, too, but you can only find so many bodies before you begin to dread the hunt.

This one was two little girls. They lived on a farm and they went missing when they were supposed to be playing in the creek near the pen with the horses. After their parents did the searching the barn thing and the calling the neighbors thing, half the town turned out to walk through the woods, ten yards apart in a horizontal line, hollering their names and shining flashlights against the black trees. Around dawn I got the call. It woke my wife up, too, but I told her to go back to sleep and I got a jug of water and a bowl for Ruckus in case he got thirsty, and I put him in his crate in the back of the truck and we drove out to the farm.

We pulled up in the wet clay driveway where a few sheriff's deputies were standing around drinking coffee. The sun was coming up red and hazy. It was chilly. That early-fall chill was everywhere, in the grass and the air, and the clouds were coming in.

"It'll rain before midmorning," one of the deputies said as I got out of the truck.

"Yeah," another one said.

I opened the wire door to Ruckus's crate and put his leash on him and let him out. He jumped down from the bed of the truck and ran into the grass, where he flopped over on his back and rolled around, kicking his feet in the air and yelping. Then he lay on his belly and looked at us, his brown and white fur spackled with dew, his ears and his tongue hanging almost to the ground. His face looked sad even as he wagged his tail.

"So it's two little girls," the first deputy said.

"I heard," I said.

"Think he can find them?"

"Yeah, he always does."

"Rain's coming in though," the deputy said, waving his coffee toward the clouds.

"We'll hurry," I said, even though it didn't matter. The rain could come down and drizzle through the scent and muddle it all up in the wet and Ruckus would still find them. He was good. I'd trained him to be good.

*First long hunt with Ruckus. I've dragged the dummy across the field, picked it up over my shoulder and walked in zigzags and put it down again. Dipped it in the lake. Carried it half a mile with no touchstone for Ruckus to get the scent. And it rained this afternoon.*

*Ruckus is smiling his dog-smile at me. He's tugging the end of the leash. He skips right over all the tricks, the traps, the snags in the trail that I've put out to test him. He pulls me at a jog through the woods, his nose in the dirt, the sun glossy on his fur. He's got it, he's got it now. He finds the dummy in the gully. He goes up and sticks his nose in it and turns around and gives exactly the right bark and wags his tail at me. And I say, "Good boy, good dog Ruckus." I give him his cookie, throw the ball for him. He bounds around, light and young.*

The parents came out of the house, the man with his arm around the woman. She had a blue shirt in her hand. She handed it to me and I knelt down and held it out to Ruckus. He stuck his nose up in it, the cold black nose wet and snuffling in the shirt and against my knuckles.

"Do you think they're okay?" the woman said. I looked up at her. Her eyes were dry and red, her mouth tight, smiling a tight smile.

I didn't say anything. Ruckus barked and stuck his nose to the ground and started wandering over toward the house, tugging at the end of the leash. He lingered at the corner of the house, near a drainpipe, then he broke into a trot, his short legs plodding in the dew-wet grass, and headed down to the horse pen. The deputies and the parents followed us.

At the pen, the three horses watched Ruckus with careful eyes. They backed away with their high-hoofed walk as he brushed his nose along the fenceposts, sat down and sniffed the air and scratched his ear for a minute, then snuffed on down to the creek. He splashed through it, the water up to his chest, and came out the other side and stopped, still. He smelled the air again. He put his nose into the dirt and grunted like a hog digging up truffles, and then he put his head up in the air and started baying with a noise that pierced and echoed around the cold dawn, and I reached down and unhooked the leash and Ruckus took off into the woods, howling and baying the whole way.

"Look at him go!" the deputy said.

"He's got the trail," I said. "Must be a pretty hot one, too."

Anytime Ruckus takes off like that, I know that he's got a hot trail, one where the scent stretches out as clear to his nose as a streak of crimson in the tall grass. When he has a weak scent, he mopes around, going in one direction and another, taking half the day to find whatever it is we're looking for. The way he was going at it that morning, I knew we would find the girls soon, in less than an hour, probably.

If he found them soon, soon enough, I could go back home and get in bed with my wife before she woke up. I could fall asleep beside her. Or try to. At least lie beside her and try not to look at whatever image ends up burned on the back of my eyelids.

*The man is no more than twenty. It's his wife, six months married–she's the Missing. She wasn't there when he got home from work. She's always there when he gets home from work.*

*He scratches Ruckus on the head. "Good looking dog," he says. He presses his thumb and forefinger against his eyes and shakes his head. His hair is dark black. Dirty, tousled. He tries to smile. "Used to have a pup looked like him. When we went hunting. Me and my dad."*

*"They're good dogs," I say.*

*"He good at this?"*

*"This is his first time. But he's good. He'll be good."*

*We're standing on the side of the highway where they found her car and Ruckus has already got it, he already smells her, and he's pulling me and I let him off and he bolts into the woods. I run after him, and I hear this man, this boy, following along behind me, his footsteps heavy but quick. I stop, turn, touch his elbow. "You should wait for us by the road."*

*"Like hell."*

*His eyes say he won't let me argue with him and I can hear Ruckus giving me the bark already so I turn and we keep running through the brush. His bark is close and loud and we come into a clearing and there she is. She's so young, and her hair is blonde with leaves in it. She's naked except for her socks. Her eyes are black bloody holes. There's deep, brown cuts all up and down her body, and her breasts are gone, leaving brown, scabby circles. Her fingers are stiff, bent at odd angles. Her mouth just slightly open.*

*Ruckus sits beside her, tail thumping, tongue lolling.*

*The man pants beside me, puts his hands on his thighs, retches. He falls down on his knees and pulls on his hair and lets out this groan that sounds like hell slipping out of his lips.*

*Other than that, the clearing is quiet. Ruckus's tail goes whump whump on the ground. I walk quiet over to him, rub his chest, under his chin. He nuzzles my hand, looking for the cookie. I reach in my pocket and give it to him. I throw the ball for him, and he yelps with joy.*

We chased the sound of Ruckus's baying through the woods. I ran fast and the deputies fell behind, but I ran faster anyway, sprinting in the thick woods, where the dark held on heavy and quiet against the dawn. I felt good about today. Then I was alone in the woods, listening to Ruckus, his barking far away in the quiet. The breeze was coming in, blowing the smell of the morning through the woods, earthy and wet and cold. Thunder rolled gently in the clouds.

Then Ruckus stopped barking, and I stood and listened. Creatures were beginning to move about, rustling and squirming in the leaves. Ruckus barked again, a different bark, controlled where his baying had been so wild. It was the found bark, the one

I'd started teaching him when he was just a squirming puppy chasing a training dummy: a repetitive, sharp bark that meant he'd found the Missing. My stomach felt tight and cold. I started running again, toward the sound, toward the place where his voice broke harsh and flat against the morning. I came out of the forest and into the fading dawn, Ruckus's barking loud and close in my ears, and ran up a hill. I could hear him and I knew that Ruckus was right on the other side of the hill with the two little girls and I sprinted across the wet ground and prayed the same prayer that I prayed a variation of every time. It's a cry for mercy, a plea; it's me begging to God that this time will be different, that this time there will be life. It's the prayer of the fireman in the ruined building, the paramedic at the head-on collision. It's the prayer that God never listens to.

# LIGHT IN THE COLD

Jerome wasn't sure how long Meredith had cheated on him. He never asked her. It could have started after the kids went away for college, or even before that. He would never have even known if he hadn't found the emails one night when she had gone for a run. She left them open on the computer, sitting right there for anyone to see them. Later, he wondered if it had been on purpose, some sort of quiet confession, or if she had had a genuine mental lapse. Regardless, they were there, all in one folder, 117 emails from a man he'd never heard of, dating back four years. He only had to read a few of them to get the gist of it. Then he left the computer and she came back from her run and he tried to think of what to say to her.

She went to work and he went to work and the kids came to visit and left. Jerome and Meredith went to bed together every night but he held it in, waited for the right time, until a few months later, before he'd even worked out how to confront her, she came home crying, inconsolable. She cried off and on for three days and refused to tell him what was wrong, said she was just stressed, and then on the fourth day she came out of her room and said that she wanted to go to Scotland.

Meredith had been saying for years that she wanted to go to Scotland. She thought it was some sort of calling; her great-great grandfather had been born there and crossed the ocean in one of those cramped cold immigrant ships. It seemed to Jerome like something that couldn't possibly matter: people that lived their whole lives and died before anyone he knew was even born. But she said it was her heritage, her children's heritage, and she owed it to herself to go. Jerome agreed to take her; he wanted to get away from the house for a while, away from the computer and away from emails, both his and hers.

So they flew into Heathrow–for both of them, the first time to leave the country–and spent less than a day in London before getting on the train to Glasgow. They shot north through England along the tracks, crossing unceremoniously into Scottish lands just before dawn. Meredith slept upright beside him with her arms crossed. Jerome wondered what she was dreaming about. He leaned his head against the window and felt the cold glass against his temple. He looked out into the field and tried to picture the battles a thousand years before, the Scots out there on those fields, fighting with pitchforks and axes against the British. Fog was coming in dark and heavy from the direction of the sea.

The last time he and Meredith had taken a trip together, just the two of them, was years and years ago, when they were just out of college, before they had their first child. They'd driven the car west, down I-10 through New Orleans and Houston all the way to San Diego. He didn't remember much about the cities they visited. What he did remember was driving across Texas at night with the moon full and heavy and the desert stretching out pale on all sides of them. The road didn't ever seem to bend. Meredith was young and he was young and she fell asleep with her head on his lap, and the world was nothing but her and the desert and the sky.

Jerome tried to remember this while the train coasted along the tracks. Every time he closed his eyes, he pictured the moon and the desert, but the road was winding like a mountain trail, and Meredith was looking out the window, constantly looking for something else out the passenger window. So Jerome kept his eyes open as the train slid north. He watched the fog charge across the field like the ghosts of soldiers rushing into the wild darkness.

Meredith woke up and they watched the sun come up over a field dotted with sheep and patches of mist. The arrived in Glasgow in late morning; they got out of the train with their backpacks, and set off to find a hotel. Meredith wanted to do it this way: traveling only with what they could carry. She had liked this roughing-it stuff more than Jerome for as long as he remembered, certainly the whole thirty years they'd been married. The bag felt heavy and hurt his back. He watched a young American traveler with the same sort of backpack trot up a staircase. We're too old to be doing this, he thought.

Glasgow didn't feel like Scotland, or not what Scotland ought to feel like, anyway. The sun was bright and reflected on the tall glass buildings. Teenage kids in clothes with the names of American bands on them hung around all of the cafes. Jerome and Meredith walked along the river, constantly shifting the loads on their backs. Across the river a giant, segmented structure humped against the horizon like a giant white beetle. Meredith asked a guy who was selling balloons what it was called. He said, "the armadillo," with a British accent, and Jerome thought that was pretty appropriate–the name, not the accent. Meredith was walking fast. It was November, cold, but Jerome was starting to sweat.

They turned down another street leading away from the river. The buildings looked ramshackle and graffiti covered the walls. Two men sat on the steps of a building with broken-out windows. They stopped talking and watched as Jerome and Meredith passed.

"Have you had enough yet?" Meredith asked.

"Yeah, let's get to a hotel."

"I mean, have you had enough of Glasgow?"

Jerome looked at her. She had a sort of mischievous look about her. "We've been here a couple of hours," he said.

"I know." They set their bags down. She put her hands on her hips and looked around, biting the inside of her lips. "I just feel like we're wasting our time. This isn't what I came to see." She waved her hand at a wall that read *wanker* in giant pink letters.

"What do you want to see?"

"I want to see whatever it is that Scottish people see. I want to feel what it's like to live here."

"Most of the people in Glasgow are Scottish."

"Don't be a smartass. I want to see what my ancestors saw, you know? Let's go up north, they were from up north."

So Jerome hefted his bag onto his back and they walked all the way back to the train station. They got pizza from a little stand near the escalators and sat down at a picnic table. Jerome pulled a map from the back pocket of his backpack and spread it out on the table. They chewed their pizza and looked at the map. Meredith took a blue marker out of her purse and circled Glasgow. She ran her finger north along the train tracks; Scotland flared out from Glasgow like a flame into the North Atlantic. The land was dotted with Burghs and Shires. Meredith rested her finger on the Ockney Islands, a clump of islands stretching like smoke between the Atlantic and the North sea. Jerome imagined the islands; he saw black water, cold black water slushed along the edges with dirty snow and ice, crashing salty against rocks and towering cliffs, trade winds spraying it high into the wild night. That felt like Scotland. So they bought tickets to Thurso, where they could catch a ferry to the wild islands.

They got on a slow train and headed north out of the city, the slummy outskirts of Glasgow trailing away behind them. The track carried them up, up out of lower Scotland, through the fields, through Perth and Inverness and into the highlands, where the grass stretched out a yellow-green on either side of them into the hills–low rounded hills covered in heather, salmon pink, and tall rocky hills that all seemed to have stopped just a little short of being mountains. The train slowed at every little town, stopping for only a minute or so before moving on: Dingwall and Invergordon, Tain and Culrain, scattered behind them like crumbs along a trail.

They went through a tunnel and came out on the other side in a valley, green with snow sitting like melted marshmallow in the low places, in the ditches alongside the tracks. The hills were high all around them and dotted with gray snow.

Meredith sat up and put her palms on the glass window. She had her nose pressed right up against the glass like a little kid. She looked eager, apprehensive. For a second, the look made Jerome feel sick; that's what she looked like in his nightmare visions of their car in the desert. He wondered if she looked like that when she went to visit the other man. But he pushed the feeling aside, as he had every other time.

The train slowed as they wove their way between the hills. There were pens of sheep, hundreds of sheep like popcorn on the grass, and they looked up and chewed silently and watched the train as it slid past. In one pen a man stood, holding a shovel. He wasn't doing anything, just standing there in the middle of all the sheep, looking off toward the hills. The train pulled into a station. The sign said *Rogart*.

"Do you think we could get off here?" Meredith asked.

"Are you serious?" Jerome said.

"Yeah. Let's get off." She stood up and grabbed her bag and started walking.

"Hey," Jerome said, getting up. He looked back at his seat and at his bag and up to Meredith, who was already opening the door to the car. "Hey, hang on." He pulled the bag from the overhead rack and it fell heavy to the floor. He lifted it onto his back and jogged after her, the pack bouncing on his shoulders. He stepped off the train and the air was crisp and cold. It smelled like sheep. Meredith was standing with her hands on her hips, smiling with her eyes closed. "Get back on," Jerome said.

"It is so beautiful here," she said. "Smell it? It even smells like Scotland!"

"It smells like sheep shit." Jerome looked at the train. An attendant was standing in the door of the train, watching them. He looked at his watch. The train hissed. "We need to get back on the train if we want to get to Thurso. If you want to go to Ockney still."

Meredith was looking around now. "Let's just stay here. I like it here."

"We don't even know if there's a hotel."

The attendant whistled and Jerome looked at him. "Coming, mate?" the attendant said.

Jerome looked at Meredith and she shook her head. The attendant nodded and went inside. The door hissed shut and the train whistled and started moving, quietly moving north to the sea while Jerome and Meredith stood on the deck at the station, watching it slide away.

The sky felt close above his head. Jerome looked up at the hard and fading blue. Around the edge of valley, clouds were hanging, low and gray and oppressive. The sun was starting to go down and the dark was coming in at them from all sides, sliding quietly down the edges of the bowl of the valley

"So what do you want to do now?" Jerome said.

Meredith didn't say anything. She started walking. Jerome looked around him. The station had apparently been turned into some sort of makeshift museum. The old ticket office stood on the other side of the tracks, a tiny blue and white building the size of a bedroom. There was a gravel walkway going down from the station and around the area in a loop. Along the trail there were lots of old railway cars: dining cars, freight cars, a couple of flatbeds, and a caboose, all sitting in the dirt with grass growing up along the sides. The doors were open. An old steam engine, red with rust, sat at the end of the trail. The place was deserted.

They could see the town a little way up the hill from the station; it wasn't anything more than a few dozen gray-roofed buildings set against the green of the highlands. They walked up the road. A man rode by on a bicycle. Meredith waved to him and he nodded. They passed stone houses and a church surrounded by tall tombstones. Jerome imagined how cold the stones must feel, how old.

The sun dipped behind the hills and the shadow came over them like someone turning off a light. The clouds were coming in faster and it was getting colder, so Jerome and Meredith sped up. They entered the town right as the few streetlights came on. The shops were closed; Meredith walked from window to window anyway, looking in: a taffy-pulling machine idle in a candy store, a mannequin sitting cross-legged in a gray suit at the tailoring shop, shovels and shearing-scissors lining shelves at the hardware store. Up ahead a door was open, a light was on.

The pub was called Jack's Lantern; the sign had a grinning brown Jack o'lantern with angry triangle eyes carved on it. Inside, it was warm and smoky, small, and quiet. There were a dozen or so men in the bar, a couple of women, and the bartender: a girl who didn't yet look eighteen. Some of the people sat together, talking in low tones. Most sat alone. Jerome and Meredith went up to the counter. Behind the bar were countless bottles of whisky. "From most every distillery in Scotland," the girl explained. Jerome read the bottles, names like Lochside and Pulteney and Aberfeldy. Jerome got a glass of Dalwhinnie on the rocks. Meredith took a whisky from Edradow.

In a corner of the bar an old man sat alone, sipping a drink and watching Jerome and Meredith. Jerome caught his eye by accident and looked away, but looked back a minute later and saw that the man was still watching them, and the man smiled and raised his drink. Jerome smiled back, and then the man was beckoning them over. Jerome squeezed Meredith by the elbow and she looked up from her drink at the man, and then they took their drinks and crossed the bar and sat down at his table.

The man sat there for a minute, smiling at them. His face was brown and wrinkled and his nose seemed way too big, as if it belonged to someone else, but his hair was black, black like a twenty-year-old's, even though he must have been past seventy.

"What you drinking?" he said.

Jerome swirled the brown liquid around in the bottom of his glass. "Whinney something," he said.

"Dalwhinnie," the man said. "A good one. A bit smoky for me. Tastes a bit like the barrel. And for you?"

"Edradow," Meredith said.

"One of my favorites. Haunting, that one is. Warm, like a good dream." He sat back and smiled. "I've tried them all, over my time. They change year to year, though. Haven't been so good lately."

Then they were quiet. The man was leaning back in his chair, smiling, his eyes closed a bit. Jerome felt like he ought to say something. "And what do you drink?" was all he could come up with.

"Kentucky bourbon," he said. "And don't even talk to me about the irony. I've tried every scotch I've seen. American bourbon's got it all beat." Then he sat up and put out his hand– small, like a woman's hand. "I'm William," he said.

Jerome shook his hand; William's grip was tight and his hand felt rough and heavy for being so small.

Jerome and Meredith introduced themselves and William bought them another round of drinks. They sat back and drank them in the corner of the room while William asked all kinds of questions about where they were from and why they were in Rogart. Meredith told him how she felt she was connecting with her family, and how Glasgow had seemed so much like America, but how Rogart felt real to her. William talked about how he came to Rogart, years ago with his wife, how they had raised sheep together until she died, how he had sold all the sheep and big sections of his land, and how he was living alone off what remained of that money. "Don't have much, don't need much," he said.

After a little while they ran out of things to say and they sat back and had their third round of drinks. At the table beside them, a man with a beard lit a pipe and the smell drifted sweet over their table. There were more people in the pub now, and the girl bartender shut the door and everything felt close and warm. The

84

lights in the place were behind orange glass in the walls, and everything had a reddish glow, like being inside a womb. People were talking; the pub hummed like an orchestra tuning up. William had his eyes closed. Jerome took Meredith's hand under the table. She squeezed his fingers and smiled at him, her eyes glowing from the alcohol. A memory flashed through the back of Jerome's mind: a night in the desert, a hotel bar outside of El Paso, Meredith holding his hand under the table while a band played Elvis cover songs.

The pub got quiet, and Jerome watched the man with the pipe and the beard stand up and take a case out from under the table. Everyone in the pub was watching him, waiting for him. The man opened the case and took out an accordion and walked to a stool at the other side of the bar. He sat down with the accordion in his lap and lit his pipe. He took a couple of puffs. The bar was silent. Then he put both hands on the accordion and let the pipe dangle from his lips and began to play.

Jerome had only heard the accordion in polka, or on sitcoms where it was a source of comic relief. This man played the accordion like it was the most precious of violins. He sat with his eyes closed, smoke from the pipe drifting around his head, creeping from his mouth down over his beard. He squeezed the accordion and coaxed the air in and out as he pressed the keys. The sound was quiet, sorrowful, and it filled the room with a thickness like the smoke from his pipe. No one spoke. The song made Jerome think of William in the field with his sheep, the train disappearing over the last of the hills to the north, the clouds sitting low over the stone and earth as they had for hundreds and hundreds of years. When the man finished playing, everyone clapped, softly though, and the man returned to his seat without playing anything else. He put the accordion away under his seat and sat down. Jerome told the bartender to bring the man a drink, and she did, and the man took it and nodded and raised the drink in their direction.

"He only plays one song a night," William said. "But he writes them himself. Actually, I think he makes them up while he's up there." He closed his eyes again. "They take me back, that they do."

Jerome watched him sit there for a minute. Around the pub, people were getting up, gathering their coats and hats and gloves. The door opened and a shot of cold swirled through the room. Jerome looked at Meredith; she nodded.

"William," she said. He opened his eyes. "Thank you so much for the drinks," Meredith went on, "We've got to find a hotel. We don't even know where we're staying yet."

"I'd be happy to let you stay at my place," William said.

Jerome felt nervous at the thought. He squeezed Meredith's hand under the table. "We wouldn't want to impose," she said.

William shook his head and stood up. "It's nothing. I don't know where else you would stay anyway. There's no hotel. Maybe that little bed and breakfast up the road, but it's a bit far. Please, it would be a pleasure."

Outside, it was cold and cloudy; snow, barely visible, fell lightly, melted on Jerome's face. The streets were empty and silent. He could feel the cold of the pavement through the soles of his shoes. They walked downhill, away from the bar and the train station, past more ancient houses of stone. "Not far," William said.

The snow stopped and the clouds parted. There was a bit of sky, blacker than the black of the clouds, and then the clouds moved back a little more and the moon came out, a little slice of silver–waning, but just bright enough to light the way when they left the main road and went down a darker, dirt road between pens of sheep. The dirt crunched and squished under their feet. To either side, the sheep bleated softly, the sound flat and hollow in the cold. The sheep looked like moon-touched cotton balls scattered around them. Jerome could see the breath coming from their mouths.

They walked for twenty minutes or so. At the end of the road the moon reflected in a little pond. Around the pond were clumps of trees and shrubs, swampy stuff. Jerome figured there was peat in there. He didn't know what peat was, but he knew they had it in Scotland, and this looked like the kind of place where peat would be. Meredith slid her hand into the crook of his elbow. She felt warm pressed against him, and he wondered if she'd walked with her other man like this, and told himself no, they could never have been this familiar, this romantic.

William's house was near the pond, built with the back of the house flush up against the outer edge of the bog. It was a small house on a lot of land, land that used to hold William's sheep. Now there was a fence close to the house, separating it from land that was somebody else's. William opened the door. "Come on in, then," he said.

They wiped their feet and walked into the house. It seemed bigger once they were inside, and it was warm: he must have a heater, Jerome thought. The place would have been nicely furnished twenty years ago. Today, everything just looked used. A granite-topped counter, a leather recliner, a red and blue checkered rug. They were worn.

"Well," William said, walking around the room, "you two can have my bed, I'll sleep out here on the couch– "

"Oh no, we wouldn't have you do that," Meredith said.

"You sure?"

"Positively."

William smiled. "Then I suppose the lady can sleep on the couch, and Jerome, you can lean that recliner way back, almost like a bed. I've got some blankets, and an extra pillow."

"That will be perfect," Jerome said. They stood in the living room for a minute, looking at the recliner, not saying anything at all. The house smelled like wood chips. William looked like he was trying to think of something to say.

"Another drink?" he said finally.

Meredith sighed and sat down on the couch. "I think I'm done. I'm just going to sit here for a minute and rest." She took her shoes off and leaned back on the couch, put her feet up on the cushions. She closed her eyes and was breathing loudly in a matter of seconds and Jerome knew she was asleep. William brought out a blanket and Jerome covered Meredith up.

"So you'll have a drink with me, then?" William said. He looked very old now, Jerome thought, eager, yet tired. Jerome nodded, and William took a bottle of bourbon from a shelf in the kitchen and went out on the back porch. Jerome followed him out there and they sat on a wooden bench, looking out over the bog. He felt the cold all the way down to his lungs as he breathed. The moon was heading toward the horizon and spilling light across the wet ground. Animals made animal sounds deep inside the bog, crickets and frogs and rodents, moving about in the cold. They had to go away soon, go to wherever it was that they went until summer.

William took a swig of the bourbon straight from the bottle and handed it to Jerome. Jerome took it and drank; it tasted sour and warm and faintly grainy. He felt it in his sinuses and his stomach. He passed it back to William. They sat there in the cold for a while, trading swigs and listening to the night. He heard Meredith shift inside. He looked at her through the window; she'd rolled to her side and bundled the blanked around her chest.

"How long you two been married?" William said.

"Thirty years," Jerome said, and he took another drink and thought about that number for a minute. "Thirty years."

"That's about how long my wife and I were married before she passed."

"I'm sorry," he said. William nodded. They were quiet for another minute. Then Jerome said, "What happened to her, I mean, if you don't mind my asking, I'm just..."

"Stroke," William said. "She was shearing, out here behind the house, and it just hit her." He took another sip of the bourbon and sighed. His breath hung in a cloud in front of his face, then drifted away. "I left her out here, talking and smiling and all that, and I went inside, and when I came out she was dead on the ground with the shears in her hand, the sheep standing there half-naked."

"I'm sorry."

"It was hard. I miss her. I miss her a lot of the time."

Jerome took the bottle. William looked at him.

"Thirty years," he said. "That's something, today. The way things are today. You've got something special, Jerome."

"I know," Jerome said. He drank. He thought he saw a light, a flash, deep and faint in the bog, but it went out and the bog was dark again. "Well, I don't know. I don't know, sometimes. Sometimes we're different, different than we used to be."

William took a drink and leaned forward with his elbows on his knees. "I'll tell you something, Jerome. I'll tell you a story, and don't take this the wrong way."

"Okay."

"My wife had an affair before she died," he said, "Back when we lived in Edinburgh. And she quit him, she quit him and we left that place and came up here. I think she only came here because when she was here she knew she wouldn't fall back in with him.

"But she never told me any of that until years after it happened. I had my suspicions, that's sure, but she never told me. And finally she did, before she died, and then it was okay. But I could see her change when we came up here, when she left him. That was the part that mattered. Her talking about it, that just came in her own time. But by then I'd already long forgiven her." He put the bottle down and looked at Jerome. "Do you follow?"

"I think so," Jerome said.

"I can tell your wife loves you. She's looking at you in all the right ways, and whatever she's not telling you, she's not telling you for the right reasons."

Jerome thought of Meredith crying in her room for days, and pressing her nose against the window of the train, and squeezing his hand under the table at a bar in El Paso or Rogart. Walking with her arm in his or in bed with her arms around him—where and when, exactly, didn't even seem to matter anymore.

William handed the bottle to Jerome. "You need to relax," he said. "If she's quit him, you're worrying's over. You've just got to let her have her time."

In the quiet an owl hooted softly, far away. Jerome shivered.

"Look," William said.

William was pointing out into the bog. Out behind the trees, just above the swampy surface, Jerome saw the flash of light again, closer this time, closer still so that he could see it not flashing but floating, a hazy ball of light bobbing along the bog.

"What is it?" Jerome said.

"A Will 'o the Wisp," William said. He stood up and walked to the edge of the porch. "My grandfather told me they were spirits, spirits of the ones we love. He said they come back to comfort us."

Jerome heard Meredith murmur something inside. He looked at her through the window. She was wrapped up tight in the blanket, her face half-buried in the pillow. A single lamp lit the room, but even through the dark Jerome could see her smiling, her lips moving a little; he could tell that she was dreaming. He pressed his fingers against the cold glass. Through the fog of the dirty windowpane, she looked beautiful as she dreamed. Jerome hoped that her dream had a hard low blue sky, and that there were sheep and there was whisky and air filled with the smell of pipe smoke and the sound of the accordion. He wanted her to dream light, guiltless and forgiven.

He turned and sat down beside William on the porch steps. They watched the Will 'o the Wisp duck and weave among the reeds. "I don't know what they are exactly, the science about them," William said. He dangled the bottle between two of his fingers. "But I like my grandfather's story. I like to believe what he said. It's a nice thought. A pleasant thought."

# PRETTY SPECIAL

Maybe people think that the speaker doesn't come on until they talk. Or until I talk. But it's on all the time. I can hear the distant rumble of the interstate, the crickets singing in the brush. And people, people in their cars.

They drive up to the speaker and their voices come through my earphones and into my head. Sometimes they are singing. Talking on the phone. Fighting with the other people in the car. I don't want to hear that. Sometimes the men flirt with me. Tell me I have a sexy voice. I don't want to hear that, either. I want them to tell me whether they want cheese on their burger so that they can pay me and leave and I can listen to the crickets again.

Tonight I can't hear the crickets because it's raining. The wind blows the water sideways smack into my little window where the drops trace slow paths down the glass. The sound is everywhere: on the window, drumming on the roof over my head, spraying off the tires on the interstate, dripping in a static-laced trickle that comes through my earphones. I hear a car rumble up to the speaker. The wobbling creak of a manual-powered window rolling down. The rain spattering on the asphalt and pinging off the roof of the car. The headlights glow down the drive thru, past my window.

Through the speaker, I hear him mumbling. The words sound distant through the rain.

"Take your order?" I say. It's late. I'm not giving him the *do you want to try a combo* spiel.

He's quiet for a moment, then he starts mumbling again. I hear *sleepy*. I hear *dark*. I hear the rain. I look up at the tiny black and white TV that projects an image of the drive thru. The camera's mounted on the roof of the building, angled so that it can see the cars. The man is in an old Civic, gray and dented. His headlights wobble behind the sheets of rain. I can't see his face.

No one else is in the drive thru. "Take your time," I say.

It's just me and Robert and Keisha left in the store at this point. Robert's doing inventory. Keisha's leaning on the front counter with her chin in her hand.

My headphones are wireless. I head back to the freezer to get another bag of french fries; we'll need at least one more batch before we close. The door to the freezer is propped open. Robert kneels inside, a blue ski jacket zipped tight around him, his breath hanging in clouds in front of his face. He looks up at me, rests a clipboard on his knee.

"Come to relieve me?" Robert says. It's hard to hear him over the rain in my ears. He's got his earphones on, too. He probably can't hear what I say, either.

"You wish," I say anyway. The cold stings my face, makes me squint. I reach past him and get the fries, head back to the front and dump them into the basket. I lower the basket into the oil and the fries pop, sizzle; frost melts off the fries and fizzes and boils.

"You there?" the man at the drive thru says to the speaker. His voice sounds like it's in the middle of my head.

"You ready to order?" I say.

He's quiet for a while. Then he says, "I'm not sure what I want yet."

I start to go through the specials, but he interrupts me.

"That's not what I mean," he says.

The rain on the roof of his car is in my head like someone shaking a can full of pennies. I look at the TV. His car is still all alone in the drive thru. I can see him, barely–a shadow leaning out the window, face close to the speaker. "What do you want, then?" I say.

"You wouldn't be interested," he says.

Keisha has her cell phone out. She's diligently mashing away at the keys, engrossed in some text-message marathon. I watch the image in the TV. "Try me," I say.

"I've never told this to anybody before," he says. His voice is rough, but it sounds low and soothing behind the rain. "Not even my wife. Certainly not my kids."

"And you're going to tell me?" I say, shaking the fries in the basket, breaking them loose from each other. "I must be pretty special."

"Oh you are, sweetie, you are," he says. Then I don't hear him. Just the rain and the steady rumble of his car's engine.

Customers come in. Three teenage boys. I feel their eyes on me. One elbows his buddy; another one of them whistles. I yell at Keisha, tell her to put the phone away and deal with them.

She sighs and slips the phone into her apron and stands behind the cash register. She stares at the boys.

The man is breathing raspy in my ears. "What you want to tell me?" I say.

He makes a strange sound, something like a cross between a sigh and a groan. "More of a confession, really," he says.

"Shouldn't you save that for church?"

"I'm way beyond church, sweetie." He chuckles a bit when he says this. His laugh sounds like the rain. It sounds like the engine of his car.

Keisha's making hamburgers for the boys. The boys are in the dining room, horsing around, trying to get my attention. They're wet from the rain, tracking water and mud all over the tile. I glare at them. "Ohhhh, she's mad!" one of them says. I take the fries out of the fryer and shake them off over the oil. Dump them into the warmer and sprinkle them with salt. Their greasy vegetable smell sticks to my skin.

The man practically whispers it. "The things I'd do to you," he says. His voice goes straight through the speaker and the earphones and my ears and hits me somewhere north of the cerebellum. There's cold electricity in my spine. The wind slams the rain against the window.

"You should order," I say.

"You know what I've done?"

"We have a special on apple pies."

"I've killed more people than you've ever met."

He does another rainwater-gasoline chuckle. I watch his shadow in the TV. He's a silhouette leaned way back in his seat. People do this. They try and screw with me. They pretend it's a war and the speaker is their radio, all *roger dodger* and *over and out*. They serenade me like they're at a karaoke bar. They say *asphinctersayswhat?* "Right," I say. "We got a murderer on our hands."

"Laugh all you want," he says.

"You should order."

"You should listen."

Robert saunters up from the back with a big grin on his face. He has his hands on his ears, pressing the earphones close to

93

his head. "You hearing this guy?" he says. I hold my finger up at him.

The man in my ears growls at me: "Can you see me up there? Up there in that camera?"

His hand comes out of the window and gives me a grainy, black and white and watery wave. The aluminum counter is cold under my fingers.

"Wish I could see you, sweetie," he says.

I grab a hold of Robert's arm. I don't even like Robert.

"You know what I do with them? After I kill them?" the man says.

"We          have          other          customers."

"I keep pieces of them. Just little things. Reminder, keepsakes, you know. I have fingers, ears, an eye. It's the prettiest little blue eye. I keep it in salt water. So it don't dry out." He breathes in and out. The sounds come through the speaker and fill me up. The engine vibrates my insides. The rain is like a river flowing through my head. The man says, real slow, "You know what I'd keep from you?"

My fingers are tight on Robert's arm. He looks at me, confused. "Take it easy," he whispers. "He's just screwing with you."

I'm clenching my teeth. "What?" I say to the man in the car.

"I'd keep your lips. You've got that voice. Voice like that, you got to have pretty lips."

Keisha is looking at me. The boys in the dining room have stopped screwing around. They're all leaning on the counter, watching me. Robert tries to pry my fingers off his arm.

"I'm going to call the police," I say.

"Don't bother all that," the man says. "I'm not after you, sweetie. I was just saying. I bet you got pretty lips. It's a compliment."

"I'm serious."

He laughs. His shadow moves in the car. "All right. Just tell me this. Am I right? Tell me what your lips look like."

There's all kinds of noise in my head, but I can tell the store is totally silent. Burgers are sizzling on the griddle. Robert's face is tight. I let go of his arm and turn my face into the corner. "I do have pretty lips," I whisper.

I can hear him smiling. It changes the frequency of the engine, resonates through the rain. "You know what," he says, "I'm not all that hungry, come to think of it. Take care, sweet thing."

The car moves in the TV screen and then its old gray hood pulls into view outside. There's water on my window and a sheet of rain between the store and the car and the man has rolled his window up and there's water on that, too. I can't see anything. I press my nose against the window and squint but it's too late; the car is past, it's just two blurry red taillights blinking their way back onto the highway.

There's nothing but rain in my ears. Robert and Keisha and the boys look at me. I lick my lips.

# ASHES OVER ST. ANDREW

My brother pulled into the spot beside me in the parking lot. He had the windows of the white sports car up, but I could still hear the music, the bass thumping through the glass. He turned the car off and got out and looked at me. I ran my hands through my hair, looked out over St. Andrew's Bay, and opened the door. The wind was strong, and hot, even though it was spring, a day before Easter. Hot even for Florida. Grains of sand skitted across the parking lot and stung like salt-shot on my skin.

"Nick," Wally said.

I nodded at him. "Hey Wally."

"Where's he supposed to be?"

"Here. He just said the yacht club."

I scanned the club. The parking lot where we flew kites when we were kids. The long green lawn where we played pickup football. The deck where our parents sat together and watched us. We'd grown up just down the road, and the yacht club was like a second home. For Wally, it still was; he'd married some woman after college and moved right back into town, practically right across the street from our parents. I had come home to live for one summer and promised I'd never do it again. Vacations only. I was just in town for the Easter weekend.

Wally was looking out over the water, the scar that notched his eyebrow forcing his right eye into a perpetual squint. He pointed. "He's out there. On the big dock."

I squinted against the sun. At the end of the concrete pier, I could see our grandfather, old and small and white-haired, sitting with his legs dangling over the open water.

We walked out to the end of the dock, past the rows and rows of boats; fishing boats raised on carpeted platforms, giant cruising sailboats bobbing in their slips. The wind blew through the masts, whistling, slapping the halyards on the wire stays with a clanking sound. The air smelled like seaweed and salt. It felt like summer out there, summer fifteen years ago. Our grandfather looked up at us and smiled when we got to the end of the dock. He held an urn in his lap, a small, curvy thing, blue, with white and gray rings painted on it.

"Hey boys," he said. Wally and I sat down on either side of him. We looked out over the water and watched a barge cruise by in the channel. "So what's up?"

"Mema told us you wanted to talk to us," Wally said.

"Yeah, yeah I do."

"You know we're coming over tomorrow, right?" I said. "We're all having Easter brunch."

"I know that," my grandfather said. He shifted the urn in his hands. "I just wanted to talk to you guys alone. Can't I do that?"

"Sure."

"And it's nice out here."

I looked out over the bay to the tree-covered peninsula on the other side, then up at the sky, the clouds skudding along past the high bright sun, and down into the water. The water crashed into the breakwater under the dock as the waves came in, then slurped back out between the cracks in the wood like a sigh as the waves receded. I felt the wind on my face. "Yeah," I said, "it's pretty nice."

"It *is* nice. And that's part of why I wanted you guys to come out here. It's a fitting background. Or backdrop. For the conversation. I revised my will the other day."

"You need to quit doing that, Grandaddy," Wally said. He was looking at his feet. "Revising the will all the time makes people think they can influence you, get you to change it in their favor. Get what they want out of you. When you die."

"I'm not screwing with that, the who's getting what," my grandfather said. "I got all that figured out years ago. And don't think either of you are getting any of it, either. It's going to your mom, and your uncle, and they can figure it out from there. So don't try and kiss my ass."

"We're not," Wally said.

"What's in the urn?" I said.

"Ashes," my grandfather said.

"Whose?"

"They're practice ashes. That's what I put in the will. Directions for the treatment of my, I guess my earthly remains. My ashes."

97

He handed me the urn. The ceramic felt light, cool in my hands.

"I'm putting you boys in charge of scattering the ashes when           I'm           dead."

"Like, half and half?" Wally said.

"No. That defeats the purpose. You got to do it together."

"Why?"

"Why do I have to tell you why? It's the final request of a dead   man.       You   can   respect   that,   right?"

"You're not dead yet," I said.

"But I will be. Someday. And when I am, I don't want you two bitching and moaning about having to do something together and end up screwing it all up. So I'm giving you forewarning. And a chance to practice."

"Fine then," Wally said. He reached across our grandfather and took the ashes from me and stood up. He took the lid off of the urn. I stood beside him and looked inside. The ashes filled the container about half way; they looked like gray sand. "Where did you get these?"

"Out of the barbeque pit," he said. He swung his feet back and forth while the waves crashed below him.

"This is stupid," I said.

"Pretend I'm not here. Pretend it's the real deal."

I put my hand on the urn beside Wally's. "Dump them out," I said.

"You're not going to say anything?" our grandfather said.

"Oh Lord," Wally said, really loudly. "Oh gracious wonderful Lord, commit our Grandaddy to your heavenly bosom. Ashes to ashes and dust and all that. Shake the urn, Nick, and get your hand off of mine."

"You're doing it here?"

We stared at our grandfather. The wind threw his hair around in crazy, wispy patterns. "Yeah?" I said.

"Well what about the wind? I'll blow back all over the boats and everything. Or get all mucked up in the breakwater. That's no way to go."

Wally tapped his foot. "We could take the Hobie," he said.

"Now you're talking," our grandfather said. "Go. Go sailing. Scatter me out good and deep. I'll watch from here."

We put the lid on the urn and left him on the end of the pier.

"You think the Hobie will still sail?" I asked.

We walked back down the dock to where we could see the spit of land, off to the side of the dock, where club members beached their boats for free. The little catamaran was sitting there, weeds and grass grown up around it, the hulls dark from mildew. "Ought to," Wally said. "I mean, I don't see why it wouldn't. Wouldn't sail."

"Well, do you even know where the sails are? And the blocks? All that?" I asked him.

"They're in the loft," he said, pointing to the hanger-like building up near the road.

I hesitated for a minute. I didn't want to get my clothes all wet, and I knew that with the size of that boat there was no way to stay dry. Sailing the Hobie in this kind of wind was like taking a top-down convertible through a carwash. And I didn't think I could stand a day on the water with Wally. But I figured my grandfather would keep guilting us until we did what he wanted. We'd just get it over with. "All right," I said.

We walked back down the dock. "It will be fun," he said. "Not like you have anyone you're trying to get home to."

I just stared at his back as he walked. The bastard.

I used to have someone to go home to. Jenny, my Jenny, my wife. My ex-wife. I'd met her in grad school, where I was going for my MBA, and she for a doctorate in anthropology. She looked like what I thought an anthropology specialist would look like: short, plain; chin-length brown hair and little round glasses. She was not gorgeous by any stretch of the imagination, and that was perfect. She was pretty enough for me, and since I knew that no one else would think so, no one would try to take her away from me.

We were married after I graduated, and I took a job as a project manager at a computer company in the town where we went to school. It was supposed to be temporary, to support Jenny while she finished up her doctorate. I still work there today.

After a few months the familiarity and routine set in; we were still very much in love, but the infatuation, the late nights of talking and the random sex on tabletops and toilet seats, had stopped. I worked and she studied and we were there and making it, together–but we were getting bored.

For her birthday I got her a computer game that a bunch of the guys at work had been talking about. It was called *Wartide*, and you played as medieval-style people and monsters and fought with other people online. Jenny used to read those weird fantasy novels about dragons and elves and all that when she was a kid, and I thought she would get a kick out of this. And I wanted to give her something to do, something that would make her forget that she was getting bored with me.

She installed the game on the desktop computer in the living room of our apartment. I pulled a chair up beside her and watched the introductory video roll; monsters and human-looking things shot fire and hit each other with swords. Jenny clapped her hands the way she does when she's excited–quickly and quietly, right in front of her face. "This looks so cool," she said. After the intro ended, the screen told her to pick her character. She picked an elf, a tall, curvaceous creature with blue skin and silver hair. "I'm a warrior," she said, pointing out the little sword and shield that her character carried.

"You *are* a warrior," I said, "That's why I love you." I kissed her on top of her head.

She named the character Honeypot. I watched her play the game for a few minutes. It consisted mostly of Honeypot running around hitting little animals with swords. After a while I left her to play while I went into the bedroom and watched TV.

There weren't any problems for a long time. Things even got better. We cooked and ate together, slept together, drank and talked on our porch, and when we'd had our fill of each other and had nothing better to do, she played her game. And this was fine, until one day I was cooking dinner while she sat in the glow of the computer. I looked at her over the onions and peppers as I chopped; she made the cutest little face–her eyes scrunched, her lips a little puckered–while she played. I finished dinner and told her so and set our plates on the table and sat down. She didn't move. "Jenny, dinner," I said.

"Hang on, hang on," she said. She was typing furiously. I sat at the table, tapping the tines of my fork against the edge of my

100

plate. Then she turned around and gave me her sad puppy dog look. "You're going to be mad," she said.

"What."

"Can I eat it over here? I can't leave the group." I just looked at her. She cocked her head. "Pleeeeease?" she said. I carried her plate over and put it on the table next to the keyboard. "I love you," she said in a singsong voice. I sat at the table alone and ate my dinner. I watched Jenny. She took a bite, now and then, but for the most part, she kept her hands on the keyboard, on the mouse.

This got worse as the months went by. The more she played, the more she had to play, and she never wanted to do anything else. I watched her play. She was scaring me a little. But she was smiling, and so excited, and happy like I hadn't seen her in a long time. So I decided to let it ride. She'd come to our bed and tell me about her latest victory, and I'd push her off and say, "You're such a nerd." And she'd laugh, and then skip back into the living room with a little whoop and sit down at the computer. "You coming to bed?" I'd ask, but she'd never answer, and I'd turn out the light and watch her through the open door until I fell asleep.

This became our routine. She came home from campus earlier and earlier. I found her in front of the computer every day when I got home from work. She asked me to cook her food that she could eat with one hand so that she didn't have to stop playing. She bought a little microphone that she plugged into the side of the computer. She talked into it, prefacing everything she said with "Hey guys, it's Honey," and then disembodied, static-scrambled voices answered her from the computer. She hardly ever came to bed with me, and when she did, the first thing she would say was always something like, "I got the Helm of Infinite Destruction," or, "We killed the Black Dragon Lord." It was everything I could do to keep from covering my head with the pillow while she talked about that shit.

I went to bed alone at night. I turned the light off and watched her, watched her through the open door. She had that same look on her face, the look that I used to think was cute, and now it made me sick. It was getting late, and she turned the living room lights off and spoke softly into the microphone. The glow from the monitor surrounded her, haloed her with greenish-white. I felt the glow inching its way into our bedroom, across my feet under our sheets, up the covers to swallow me whole.

That night, Jenny woke me up. "We need to talk," she said. I rolled over and looked at her. "All right," I said.

"No, get up. This is important." She went out into the living room and sat down in the computer chair and swivelled it away from the monitor, toward the kitchen table. I got out of bed and put my sweatpants on. Then I went into the kitchen and got a beer from the fridge. I offered one to Jenny and she shook her head, so I opened mine and sat down at the kitchen table. I took a sip. Then she said, "I think we need some time apart."

I swished the beer in my mouth and held it. Then I swallowed it. I looked at her; she wasn't smiling, wasn't laughing. I tapped my finger on the neck of the bottle. "You're serious?" I asked her.

"Yes."

I drank some more of my beer. "Why?"

She shrugged. "I don't know, I just, I feel like, like the spark is gone, you know? We don't play the way we used to. How long has it been since we made love?"

"Seventeen days."

"See!" she said. "That's not how it should be. And I need to get my life sorted out, too." She looked sort of ashamed, then she looked at the ground. "I've had to postpone defending my dissertation. Another year."

I slammed my beer on the table. "Another year? You told me you were close, you were almost ready. This was months ago you told me! How long do you expect me to work this shitty job, waiting for you to get your damn degree?"

"It's hard," she said. I could see that she was starting to cry. "I'm just so busy all the time, there's so much work to do –"

"I never see you work." And it was true, I hadn't seen her doing a bit of work since, well, since her birthday.

"What do you think I do on campus all day?" She was crying now. I picked my beer back up and drank a lot of it. "And there's something else," she said quietly.

I felt my stomach knot. "What."

"I've met someone."

"You're cheating on me."

"No! Never, I wouldn't." She was full-fledged bawling now, her eyes red and bloodshot, tears smearing the little bit of makeup she wore. The computer glowed behind her, silhouetting her head, her hair. "I've never met him in real life."

I looked at her, at her drowning eyes. The computer hummed. "You've got to be kidding me," I said.

She put her face in her hands. I got up and slid her chair out of the way. Honeypot stood on the screen wearing all kinds of glowing armor. In front of her, another character, one that looked like a midget in a robe, was dancing that Russian folk dance, the one where they cross their arms and kick their feet out in front of them. The character's name hovered above his head: Holyrage. On the bottom of the screen were lines of text:

Honeypot whispers: he's here. one sec

Holyrage whispers: k

Holyrage whispers: Honeybunny?

Holyrage whispers: hellooooooo?

I looked at her and she was not looking at me, she was looking at the screen. Her hands were tightly folded in her lap. "His name's Jacob," she said. "He's–"

"I don't even want to know." I went back into the bedroom and shut the door.

I found her sleeping on the couch when I woke up the next morning. She still had her clothes on, and she'd taken towels from the closet and put them across her like blankets. I took the blanket off our bed and spread it over her, then I kissed her on the forehead. "We'll get through this," I whispered to her. "I love you too much for this." She murmured something and rolled over, pulling the blanket tight around her.

I went to work. When I got home, Jenny and the computer were gone.

Wally took the padlocks off the door to the sail loft and lifted the door. It went up haltingly, like an automatic garage door whose gears were slipping. The light came in from behind us and painted the walls and the cold concrete floor a pale yellow. Inside, it smelled like a worn pair of gardening gloves. Some old, single-person dinghies sat in the middle of the loft. Along either wall were dozens of racks of sails in all different sizes, all different colors. In the bottom row in the very back corner, beneath a couple of newer sails, I found the sail to the Hobie. Wally found the rest of the gear in a locker, the tiller and the blocks and the butt-buckets–harnesses that clip you onto the trapeze so that you can put your weight way, way out over the water to keep the boat flat–and we carried it all outside and set it down beside the boat. I took my shirt and my shoes off and rolled up my jeans. The grass felt cool between my toes.

We dragged the bows of the boat around so that they were facing out toward the bay, straight into the wind. Wally climbed onto the tramp, the mesh surface that connected the two hulls and served as the only place to sit while sailing. He unwrapped the sail enough to find the top. Then he untied the halyard from the mast and clipped it to the eye in the top of the sail, and while I fed the luff of the sail into the groove in the mast, Wally pulled hard on the halyard, hand over hand, raising the sail toward the sky. There was a smell of mold coming from the sail, and as it unfurled, a few cockroaches fell out onto the tramp. I jumped back and watched them skitter away into the grass. The sail went up, and the sun hit it, and the colors, panels of blue and purple fading into red and back again into blue, looked as bright and clean as they had when we'd last taken the boat on the water together, over ten years ago.

"I'm skipper," Wally said.

"Like hell. I'll steer," I said.

Wally took the urn and jammed it into the lacings that held the tramp to the hulls. He wiggled it and tugged a little. It looked secure. Then he took off all of his clothes except for his shorts and put on a butt-bucket and tossed the other one to me. I put it on and we each grabbed a hull and pulled toward the water. The vines that had grown around the hulls over the years popped and snapped as we pulled. We reached the water's edge and my feet hit the first of the waves. It was freezing. "Shit," I said.

"Yeah, hope we don't flip," Wally said.

"I won't flip us."

"You might. Might be you're not as hot-shit as you think." He looked at me; his eyes were glaring and his nose was twitching a little.

104

We gave the boat another tug and then it was floating, and Wally climbed on and trimmed the jib in tight, and then I gave the boat one more push and got on and pushed the rudders down. I sat cross-legged and steered us out past the end of the dock, where our grandfather sat waving to us. I aimed the hulls out into the open water, and we were sailing.

I had forgotten what it feels like, to steer the boat and control the sail, to feel the water in one hand and the wind in the other. I sailed straight out from shore, beating very close to the wind, the sail in tight. Wally adjusted the jib and sat down beside me. The wind ripped along the sail and across our faces. We had raced this boat together, years and years ago, with me as skipper and him as crew. We didn't have to tell each other where to sit, what to do. It was totally natural. The boat slid through the water, bobbing a bit on the waves, splashing us with drops that felt like salty ice when the hulls came down too hard. I watched a puff of wind coming towards us, a darker spot of wrinkles on the blue of the bay, and let the sail out a little as it hit us.

Wally tested the ashes again; they were holding firm, wedged in the lacing. "So should we do it here?" Wally asked.

I sailed along, feeling the boat rise and fall on the little swells. "You really want to do it yet?" I said. "We could sail a little more first. I bet we can haul ass today, wind like it is."

Wally grinned. "It's blowing like stink!"

"It's blowing dogs off chains!" I said, and then I fell off the wind a bit, put us on a reach, the wind blowing straight at our backs, pushing the boat as fast as it would go. We started to heel over a bit, and we both scooted our butts out to the very edge of the tramp. The boat continued to lean; I felt the hull underneath us rise a little out of the water and come splashing down again. "You're going to have to go out," I said.

"All right," Wally said. He grabbed the clip on the trapeze and clipped it into the hook on the front of his butt-bucket. Then, holding onto the handle on the trapeze, he bent his knees and put his feet on the hull and stood up and leaned all the way back, the complicated system of lines and blocks and bungees holding his weight as he stretched straight out over the water. The boat flattened out for a second.

"Whooooooooo!" Wally was cheering, the salt-spray wetting his face.

The boat started to heel again, and I didn't want to let the sail out and slow down, so I clipped into the other trapeze, and, holding onto the tiller and the mainsheet, stepped out beside Wally. And for a few minutes we hung there, side-by-side and horizontal above the blue with the bay erupting in spray around the hulls and coating us and the wind blowing the salt smell everywhere everywhere and the speed! The hulls were pitching forward as the wind slammed gust after gust into the sail. We both took a step toward the stern. We picked up speed and the boat pitched forward again, the leeward hull almost buried under the rush of water.

"You're going to pitch-pole us!" Wally yelled.

"So take another step back," I said, and before I could step back or he could step back the leeward hull buried, and the boat went from blinding rushing speed to dead in the water in about half a second. Wally and I kept going, momentum hurling him, still attached to the trapeze, around the sidestay, the forestay, pulling the mast further toward the water the whole time, until he landed on his back in the jib, and a second later I landed on top of him, and then our weight on the mast was more than it could take and the mast came down into the water, pulling the hulls with it, and the boat came to rest on its side, capsized in the middle of the bay.

The first time that I met Wally's wife was the night before their rehearsal dinner. Like Jenny and me, Wally and Rebecca had a short courtship; their wedding was only six weeks after he announced that he had a serious girlfriend. This had caught everyone in our family by surprise. Wally had never had a serious girlfriend. He'd gone through high school and college single, spending most of his time studying and drinking. Even after he graduated, when got his degree in architecture and took a job at a firm that earned him all kinds of money, he remained alone. Then he met Rebecca, and apparently *she* proposed to *him*, and thinking back on it, maybe we shouldn't have been so surprised when he said yes. She fell into his lap.

My flight was delayed, and I didn't get in until close to nine. I went straight to the restaurant, where everyone was supposed to meet Rebecca for the first time. When I came in, the table where my family had obviously sat was empty, and I saw them sitting at the bar: Wally and Rebecca, my parents, and my grandfather. Wally stood up when he saw me. "He's here!" he said, and walked over to me, stumbling a little. He smelled like whisky as he shook my hand. "Come meet her," he said, "you're going to love her."

Rebecca shook my hand like she was cracking a whip. She was gorgeous, in fact, with dark black hair and pale skin, a long, curvy body that showed through the skimpy dress she wore. She held a cigarette in her other hand. Wally didn't smoke.

I gave hugs all around, to my parents and to my grandfather, and we sat and talked about the rehearsal dinner and the wedding and the honeymoon plans. Rebecca kept fooling with Wally's hair, messing with his tie. When we ended up talking about family and inside jokes, I could see Rebecca smiling politely, completely lost, and Wally was trying hard to keep her involved, saying things like, "Right Bec?" She wasn't contributing much to the conversation. The most that she said came when Wally started to tell us all about the time he got arrested in high school for driving with no pants, and Rebecca simply said, "Shut up, Wally. No one wants to hear that stupid story."

After a while the rest of them got up, leaving Wally and me at the bar. Rebecca shook my hand again and said, "It was so nice to meet you," and then she put her cigarette out in her glass of wine and set it on the bar and they all left. And if I had to think of something that defined Rebecca, that was it. She was *exactly* the kind of person who leaves a bent cigarette butt floating and drizzling ashes in half a glass of warm red wine.

Wally sipped his drink and looked at me. "What do you think?" he said.

"Honestly?"

"Of course."

"Honestly, I don't know. I don't know her that well."

"First impression, then." Wally sounded desperate, eager.

"First impression, not so good. I don't know what it is," I said, "I guess you know her better than any of us do, though. You can be the judge."

"Mom and Dad don't like her."

"No?"

"They think she just wants to get married and divorce me, take my money. They want me to have a prenup written up."

"Might not be a bad idea," I said.

Wally put his drink down. "Of all people, I thought you'd be on my side."

"You do tend to rush into things."

"You're one to talk."

"It was different with Jenny."

"How?"

"Well, first of all, Jenny wasn't such a bitch," I said. I watched the bartender wash glasses at the other end of the bar. I felt Wally's eyes on me.

"You can't talk like that about her," he said.

"You're right, sorry. Maybe bitch wasn't the right word. Controlling, maybe. The word 'whipped' comes to mind." He was silent, just staring at me. "I mean, seriously," I went on, "what was all that shit, her fooling with your hair and all, constantly, and her not wanting you to tell that story?"

"It's a juvenile story–"

"You love that story! We all love that story!" I laughed. "I don't know what her motives are, or if she has motives, or hell, maybe you two are really in love. It just doesn't look like love to me."

"What do you know about love? You're fucking divorced."

"Let's not talk about my marriage," I said.

"You mean your failed marriage. The one where she decided she liked a video game more than she liked you."

I grabbed him by his collar and he knocked his glass over. The bartender looked over at us. I whispered to Wally, "I told you that in confidence. As far as everyone else knows, she just cheated on me, and that was that. I don't want this video game shit brought up again." I let him go. "You haven't told anyone, have you?"

"No," Wally said.

"Do you promise?" I said. He was quiet. His eyes were watering, intense, nervous. "Promise me," I said.

"Maybe if you weren't such an asshole, such a huge fucking asshole, maybe you wouldn't have lost your wife to a goddam computer game."

"I can't believe you," I said. I got up. "I hope you're happy with your little gold-digging slut, you son of a bitch."

I didn't go to the rehearsal dinner.

I arrived at the wedding right as it started. My dad was at the front of the aisle, standing where the best man stands, where I was supposed to be standing. I sat down beside my mother.

The reception was held at a hotel near the beach. I drank a beer at a table with some bridesmaids and watched my brother and his wife dancing. The bridesmaids clucked and giggled at each other, and one of them asked me to dance, and it was all I could do to force a smile as I said, "Thanks, but no." The bridesmaids all got up and found dancing partners and left me alone at the table with my beer. I watched them dance. On the other side of the ballroom, my grandfather leaned against the bar, the white hair on the back of his head as bright as beach sand in the sun. I skirted around the dance floor and sat down beside him and ordered another beer.

He put his hand on my back. "Glad you came today," he said. He smiled at me, and I nodded. "We missed you at the rehearsal."

"Yeah, I just got caught up."

"You don't have to bullshit. Your brother told me what happened, about your fight and all."

"Ah," I said. The bartender brought my beer and I drank. We sat in silence for a minute. The band was playing "Margaritaville." I think it was the same Jimmy Buffett cover band that had played at my wedding. It seemed like lifetimes ago.

"I agree with you, about his wife," my grandfather said. "I think she's going to fuck him and leave him and take him for everything he has." He sipped his drink, which looked like vodka on the rocks, but might have been gin, or maybe water. "But he doesn't want to hear it from us. He's stubborn like that. Going to have to learn this one the hard way."

"Maybe so."

"Hell, it might work out."

I finished my beer and signaled the bartender for another. "I just don't see why he couldn't take the advice, or the criticism, whatever you want to call it. And I especially don't see why he had to bring up Jenny."

My grandfather looked at me and he looked very old, as old as I've seen him. "You want to know why he brings that up?" I nodded. He swiveled in his chair and looked out over the crowd. "Look at him," he said. "He's not much to look at."

I looked at Wally out there on the dance floor, trying to dance, looking more like a fool than anything else. He was stumbling along, sweating; his tux didn't fit him right. Rebecca was smiling and humoring him, nonetheless.

"You've been the first or the best at everything that either of you has ever done. You're better-looking. You're an adult now and I'm allowed to tell you that. You're better-looking, and best as I can tell smarter, and you win, you win all the time where he loses. He's always been in your shadow." He paused for a minute then, and he finished his drink. Then he went on. "Except in your marriage. It's the one thing that he found where you've failed. You've failed, and he's in the middle of succeeding. And whether he means to or not, it's only natural for him to want to rub it in your face."

As old as my grandfather looked, saying this to me, he had never struck me before as being so young. He didn't seem like my grandfather, but rather another man, just another man. The age was gone, and he was telling me the truth. I felt too many emotions to sort out, and I tried to respect what he said, and to understand how things were for Wally, but inside of me, I felt it building up, anger, rage, that he would want to "rub it in my face."

"About Jenny," my grandfather said. I squeezed the bottle of beer. "Wally told me about the video game. About why she left you."

I felt the muscles in my calves tensing. My eyes watered and burned. My grandfather's face was close to mine now, and I could smell his breath; his drink was definitely vodka. "He told you," I said.

"Yeah, he's told a lot of people. I think it might be better for you to just come clean and tell everyone yourself. Might even make you feel better, get past this whole thing."

110

I wasn't even listening to him anymore. I felt like I was sweating through my suit. "He's told a lot of people," I repeated, to him, to myself, to whoever was listening, and I felt a weird mixture of anger and embarrassment, like I wanted to throw my bar stool at my reflection in the mirror behind the bar.

And that's exactly when my brother came up behind me, stumbling drunk, and said, "How's my favorite divorcé?" and I swung around and stood up in one motion and with everything I had put my fist right between his eyes. It was like slow motion: my knuckles were lined up vertically from the middle of his nose to above his eyebrows, and when I connected his face practically exploded; I bloodied his nose and split his eyebrow right along the eye socket, and he fell hard on his back and tried to get up but fell back down, and the music stopped and everyone stared and my hand was starting to hurt and I left him on his ass on the edge of the dance floor, blood spilling onto the white of his shirt.

The water was cold to the point where it was hard to breathe. I unclipped from the trapeze and floated. Wally floated beside me, quiet for a minute. Then he said, "You should have let me skipper."

I didn't say anything. I was looking for something and I didn't know what it was. I was looking at the lacings of the tramp, the empty lacings of the tramp, and then I remembered. "Oh shit," I said, and then I dove down, swam all the way to the bottom, a good 20 feet. The water was dark and unbearably cold at the bottom. I could only see a few feet in any direction. My eyes were burning from the salt and my lungs needed air. I surfaced. Wally was still just bobbing there beside the boat. "The ashes," I said, panting, and Wally's eyes got wide and he dove under. I went under again, down to the bottom, and swam along, sliding my hands over the loose sand. I was running out of air, about to swim to the top, when I saw it, the blue and white of the urn, the current knocking it end over end along the bottom like a football after kickoff. I grabbed it and swam up.

Wally surfaced a few seconds later. "Oh shit," he said, "Oh shit."

"It's not a big deal," I said. "It's barbeque ashes. We won't flip when we do it for real."

"He asked us to do one thing. One thing, and we couldn't do it. You should have let me skipper."

I paddled with my legs, holding the urn out of the water, over to the boat. I climbed up onto the starboard hull and sat down, the tramp and the sail at my back, the other hull dripping water onto my head. Wally climbed up beside me. I handed him the urn. He shook it; it sloshed like a bottle of coke. He opened the lid a crack and turned the urn on its side and let the water run out of it. When the water stopped, he took the lid off completely and set it down beside him. Then he turned the urn upside down. Dark gray drips fell in little splotches on his palm, and then the first clump of ashes slid from the urn like wet grout and plopped into his hand. He righted the urn and put the lid back on it, then he crunched the mottled ashes in his fingers and let them fall into the water. They sank slowly, like diving submarines. We floated for a minute on the bottom hull of the capsized boat in the middle of St. Andrew's Bay.

"Okay," I said finally, "let's right the boat."

It takes a lot to right a capsized catamaran. If the sails aren't uncleated, they will hold water, and the boat will never come upright. If you don't have at least 280 pounds pulling on the righting line, the boat will never come upright. This used to be a problem when we were kids. Together we weighed much more than that now. Today, we could right it.

I swam around and loosened the sails while Wally stood up on the hull and pulled the righting line out from under the tramp. I climbed up beside him and grabbed hold of the line. My knuckles lined up right beside his. He pulled with his right hand, held tight to the urn with his left. We leaned back, and at first it seemed as if nothing was happening. We were pressed together, our weight together in one wet mass, leaning toward the water. Then we felt a tiny bit of motion, and looking to the tip of the sail, I saw the mast rise an inch, then six inches, then two feet out of the water. Once the sail started to come out into the air, the top hull began to fall under its own weight, and in a few more seconds of pulling Wally and I splashed together into the cold water and the hull came down on top of us. The bows swung around into the wind and we climbed onto the boat. The sail luffed and flagged and sprinkled us with water. We sat there and caught our breath.

"So what should we do now?" Wally said.

"I don't know." The sun was warm and it felt good to sit, to dry out.

"Should we spread them out on the tramp or something? Let them dry?" He had opened the urn again and was poking his finger around in the ashes. "They're all wet. They're not going to scatter right."

I looked over at Wally and up at the colors on the sail and back at Wally again. "I don't think he really cares about the scattering."

Wally looked off into the distance and nodded. "Probably not why he wants us out here."

"Probably not."

We caught the wind in the sail and turned the boat around, back toward the shore, towards the dock and the yacht club. We sat side-by-side on the stern end of the tramp, between the hulls. Going downwind, the boat sailed smoothly, easily; I didn't even really need to steer. The wind carried us where we needed to go. The sun was warm and we dangled our feet in the water. I held the tiller lightly and headed toward the tiny figure of our grandfather waiting on the end of the dock. Wally held the urn upside down over the water, his hands awkward and rough on the smooth ceramic, the ashes sliding out in big smooth dollops. The ashes hit the water a clump at a time, like giant gray raindrops, and we watched them drift away in our wake.

# BLUE MORNING DARK

There was a man in our town who was trying to commune with nature. He had walked out of his office one day and taken off his tie and his jacket and his shoes, and he walked out of the business district and past the lines of houses in the stucco neighborhoods and up to the top of a grassy hill on the outside of town, where he sat down in his Dockers and his undershirt and looked out to the west, out to the woods where the sun was still burning hot in the afternoon.

He sat there looking at the dark woods with his hands on his knees, day and night, and his friends brought him food and drink, and he got up from time to time and walked down the hill and into the woods, which is where he went to do his business, we supposed.

It wasn't long before he was a town fixture. People besides his friends brought him food. They showed him off to visitors– *there's the mall, there's the botanical gardens, there's the man who's trying to commune with nature.* They'd try to talk to him at the top of the hill, ask him if he'd done it yet, if he'd communed with nature, and he'd say, "Still working on it."

He went up there when I was young. My dad wouldn't let me talk to him. "Don't you go anywhere near that hippie," he'd say. "He's up to no good up there. It don't do a person right to spend his days alone, up on a damn hill, relying on everyone else to feed him. No sir, you stay away from him."

When I was twelve, my friends dared me to talk to the man on the hill. I wasn't going to, but then they double-dog dared me, so I had to. I walked up the hill. This was still early in the day and the grass was wet with dew. The man was sitting cross-legged, looking out over the woods. His shirt was dirty. He'd torn the legs off of his Dockers so that they were like a pair of shorts. He reached into a basket that was sitting beside him and pulled out an apple and started eating it. There was a bird, a woodpecker, sitting on his shoulder, and it flew away when it saw me coming. I walked up to him and said hi.

He looked at me. "Hi," he said.

Then I didn't know what to say, so I said, "They dared me to come up here."

"You better have something good to tell them when you get back, then."

"Yeah."

He drummed his fingers on his knee and looked out over the woods. "What do you think is out there?" he said.

"I don't know. Trees. Animals."

He kept looking. "Tell your friends that I smelled bad," he said, and I left.

My friends didn't believe that I'd talked to him. My dad found out, though, and he believed it, and he grounded me for two weeks.

The man stayed on the hill. I didn't go out there again for six more years.

On the morning that I was going to leave for college, I woke up before dawn because I could hear my parents yelling at each other.

"We're not going out there," my dad said.

"I'm seeing this," my mom said, "I've been waiting fifteen years to see this. Don't you try and stop me." Then I heard her walking toward my room, and she opened the door and shook me even though I was already awake and she said, "He's about to do it."

"Do what?" I asked.

"Commune with nature."

"How do you know?"

"I can see it," she said. She went to the window and pulled open the curtains. "Out there in the sky."

I got dressed and my mom and I went outside into the blue morning dark. We got into the car and were pulling out of the driveway when we saw my dad coming out of the house, pulling on his coat, so we stopped and let him in the back seat.

"If that damn hippie's finally going to get off that hill," he said, "that might be something worth seeing."

We drove over to the edge of town where the hill was and pulled over on the side of the road. We had to park a long way away because most of the town was there already; the cars lined the road, bumper to bumper on either side. The crowd stood around the hill, looking up at the man, leaving a clearing around him like an old man's bald spot. When we got close I could see that there were animals all around him: a bunch of birds and squirrels, three raccoons, a turtle, and a deer with a huge rack of antlers. The man had his hands on top of his head.

"Damn hip-" my dad said, but everyone turned around and glared at him, so he shut up, and we stood there, totally silent.

The sky to the east was orange and red, and the birds were starting to make noise as the sun came up. The night was still pooled heavy and blue in the woods, but the man was facing east now, his eyes closed. The wind was coming in, getting stronger. A woman held her hat down on top of her head. The wind blew harder. I could hear it coursing through the trees, shaking the leaves with a sound like white water. The birds were getting louder and the wind was getting louder and the sun was about to breach the horizon but over it all we could hear the man; he was singing. He was singing a song none of us had heard before at the top of his voice while the crowd and the animals stood watching him and the wind blew and blew.

Then the first sliver of sun broke over the trees and the crowd watched the man while the sun painted them with orange, and the man's skin became tinged with gold, as if the light had hit him and liquefied and coated him like oil. The outline of his body seemed to wobble, and as the wind screamed across the top of the hill and into the crowd, the man began to come apart; bits of him, tiny particles like sand, began to break off and blow into the crowd. A woman beside me smiled and batted pieces of him–pale and white as flour–away from her eyelashes. The man stopped singing and the wind slowly and gracefully took flecks of him away into the sky. When the wind started to die the man was nothing but a skeleton, and that came apart, too, and the last breath of the wind wafted the dust of his bones over the tops of our heads.

The animals stood there and looked at us for a minute, then they wandered off toward the woods. The sun was up now, an orange ball hovering just above the horizon. There was nothing left of the man but a pair of cutoff Dockers and a dirty undershirt.

The crowd started to break apart. My mom put her hand on my shoulder.

116

My dad looked at me and up at the top of the hill and back down at me again. "Hey," he said, "You didn't get any of him on you, did you?"

# ABOUT THE AUTHOR

Brock Adams grew up in Panama City, Florida, and received his BA in English from the University of Florida in 2005. He went on to study fiction at the University of Central Florida, where he received his MFA in Creative Writing. He currently lives with his wife in Spartanburg, South Carolina, where he teaches English at the University of South Carolina Upstate. His fiction has received numerous commendations and awards and has been published in a variety of journals. *Gulf* is his first collection of short stories.